The Golden Flower Pot

By

E. T. A. Hoffmann

British Library Cataloguing-in-Publication Data
A catalogue record for this book is available from the
British Library

Contents

E. T. A. Hoffman

Ernst Theodor Wilhelm Hoffmann was born in Königsberg, East Prussia in 1776. His family were all jurists, and during his youth he was initially encouraged to pursue a career in law. However, in his late teens Hoffman became increasingly interested in literature and philosophy, and spent much of his time reading German classicists and attending lectures by, amongst others, Immanuel Kant.

In was in his twenties, upon moving with his uncle to Berlin, that Hoffman first began to promote himself as a composer, writing an operetta called Die Maske and entering a number of playwriting competitions. Hoffman struggled to establish himself anywhere for a while, flitting between a number of cities and dodging the attentions of Napoleon's occupying troops. In 1808, while living in Bamberg, he began his job as a theatre manager and a music critic, and Hoffman's break came a year later, with the publication of Ritter Gluck. The story centred on a man who meets, or thinks he has met, a long-dead composer, and played into the 'doppelgänger' theme – at that time very popular in literature. It was shortly after this that Hoffman began to use the pseudonym E. T. A. Hoffmann, declaring the 'A' to stand for 'Amadeus', as a tribute to the great composer, Mozart.

Over the next decade, while moving between Dresden, Leipzig and Berlin, Hoffman produced a great range of both literary and musical works. Probably Hoffman's most well-known story, produced in 1816, is 'The Nutcracker and the Mouse King', due to the fact that – some seventy-six years later - it inspired Tchaikovsky's ballet The Nutcracker.

In the same vein, his story 'The Sandman' provided both the inspiration for Léo Delibes's ballet Coppélia, and the basis for a highly influential essay by Sigmund Freud, called 'The Uncanny'. (Indeed, Freud referred to Hoffman as the "unrivalled master of the uncanny in literature.")

Alcohol abuse and syphilis eventually took a great toll on Hoffman though, and – having spent the last year of his life paralysed – he died in Berlin in 1822, aged just 46. His legacy is a powerful one, however: He is seen as a pioneer of both Romanticism and fantasy literature, and his novella, Mademoiselle de Scudéri: A Tale from the Times of Louis XIV is often cited as the first ever detective story.

First Vigil

On Ascension Day, about three o'clock in the afternoon in Dresden, a young man dashed through the Schwarzthor, or Black Gate, and ran right into a basket of apples and cookies which an old and very ugly woman had set out for sale. The crash was prodigious; what wasn't squashed or broken was scattered, and hordes of street urchins delightedly divided the booty which this quick gentleman had provided for them. At the fearful shrieking which the old hag began, her fellow vendors, leaving their cake and brandy tables, surrounded the young man, and with plebian violence scolded and stormed at him. For shame and vexation he uttered no word, but merely held out his small and by no means particularly well-filled purse, which the old woman eagerly seized and stuck into her pocket.

The hostile ring of bystanders now broke; but as the young man started off, the hag called after him, "Ay, run, run your way, Devil's Bird! You'll end up in the crystal! The crystal!" The screeching harsh voice of the woman had something unearthly in it: so that the promenaders paused in amazement, and the laughter, which at first had been universal, instantly died away.

The Student Anselmus, for the young man was no other, even though he did not in the least understand these singular phrases, felt himself seized with a certain involuntary horror; and he quickened his steps still more, until he was almost running, to escape the curious looks of the multitude, all of whom were staring at him. As he made his way through the crowd of well-dressed people, he heard them muttering on all sides: "Poor young fellow! Ha! What a vicious old witch!" The mysterious words of the old woman, oddly enough, had given this ludicrous adventure a sort of sinister turn; and the youth, previously unobserved, was now regarded with a certain sympathy. The ladies, because of his fine figure and handsome face, which the glow of inward anger rendered still more expressive, forgave him his awkwardness, as well as the dress he wore, though it was at variance with all fashion. His pike-gray frock was shaped as if the tailor had known the modern style only by hearsay; and his well-kept black satin trousers gave him a certain pedagogic air, to which his gait and manner did not at all correspond.

The Student had almost reached the end of the alley which leads out to the Linkische Bath; but his breath could no longer stand such a pace. From running, he took to walking; but he still hardly dared to lift an eye from the ground, for he still saw apples and cookies dancing around him, and every kind look from this or that pretty girl seemed to him to be only a continuation of the mocking laughter at the Schwarzthor.

In this mood he reached the entrance of the Bath: groups of holiday people, one after the other, were moving in. Music of wind instruments resounded from the place, and the din of merry guests was growing louder and louder. The poor Student Anselmus was almost ready to weep; since Ascension

Day had always been a family festival for him, he had hoped to participate in the felicities of the Linkische paradise; indeed, he had intended even to go to the length of a half portion of coffee with rum and a whole bottle of double beer, and he had put more money in his purse than was entirety convenient or advisable. And now, by accidentally kicking the apple-and--cookie basket, he had lost all the money he had with him. Of coffee, of double or single beer, of music, of looking at the pretty girls-in a word, of all his fancied enjoyments there was now nothing more to be said. He glided slowly past; and at last turned down the Elbe road, which at that time happened to be quite empty.

Beneath an elder-tree, which had grown out through the wall, he found a kind green resting place: here he sat down, and filled a pipe from the Sanitätsknaster, or health-tobacco-box, of which his friend the Conrector Paulmann had lately made him a present. Close before him rolled and chafed the gold-dyed waves of the fair Elbe: on the other side rose lordly Dresden, stretching, bold and proud, its light towers into the airy sky; farther off, the Elbe bent itself down towards flowery meads and fresh springing woods; and in the dim distance, a range of azure peaks gave notice of remote Bohemia. But, heedless of this, the Student Anselmus, looking gloomily before him, flew forth smoky clouds into the air. His chagrin at length became audible, and he said, "In truth, I am born to losses and crosses for all my life! That, as a boy, I could never guess the right way at Odds and Evens; that my bread and butter always fell on the buttered side-but I won't even mention these sorrows. But now that I've become a student, in spite of Satan, isn't it a frightful fate that I'm still as bumbling as ever? Can I put on a new coat without getting grease on it the first day, or without tearing a cursed hole in it on some nail or other? Can I ever bow to a Councillor or a lady without pitching the hat out of my hands, or even slipping on the smooth pavement, and taking an embarrassing fall? When I was in Halle, didn't I have to pay three or four groschen every market day for broken crockery-the Devil putting it into my head to dash straight forward like a lemming? Have I ever got to my coflege, or any other place that I had an appointment to, at the right time? Did it ever matter if I set out a half hour early, and planted myself at the door, with the knocker in my hand? Just as the clock is going to strike, souse! Some devil empties a wash basin down on me, or I run into some fellow coming out, and get myself engaged in endless quarrels until the time is clean gone.

"Ah, well. Where are you fled now, you blissful dreams of coming fortune, when I proudly thought that I might even reach the height of Geheimrat? And hasn't my evil star estranged me from my best patrons? I had heard, for instance, that the Councillor, to whom I have a letter of introduction, cannot stand hair cut close; with an immensity of trouble the barber managed to fasten a little queue to the back of my head; but at my first bow his unblessed knot comes loose, and a little dog which had been snuffing around me frisks off to the Geheimrat with the queue in its mouth. I spring after it in terror, and stumble against the table, where he has been working while at breakfast; and cups, plates, ink-glass, sandbox crash to the floor and a flood of chocolate and ink covers the report he has just been writing. 'Is the Devil in this man?' bellows the furious Privy Councillor, and he shoves me out of the room.

"What did it matter when Conrector Paulmann gave me hopes of copywork: will the malignant fate, which pursues me everywhere, permit it? Today even! Think of it! I intended to celebrate Ascension Day with cheerfulness of soul. I was going to stretch a point for once. I might have gone, as well as anyone else, into the Linkische Bath, and called out proudly, 'Marqueur, a botde of double beer; best sort, if you please.' I might have sat till far in the evening; and moreover close by this or that fine party of well-dressed ladies. I know it, I feel it! Heart would have come into me, I should have been quite another man; nay, I might have carried it so far, that when one of them asked, 'What time is it?' or 'What is it they are playing?' I would have started up with light grace, and without overturning my glass, or stumbling over the bench, but with a graceful bow, moving a step and a half forward, I would have answered, 'Give me leave, mademoiselle! it is the overture of the Donauweibchen'; or, 'It is just going to strike six.' Could any mortal in the world have taken it ill of me? No! I say; the girls would have looked over, smiling so roguishly; as they always do when I pluck up heart to show them that I too understand the light tone of society, and know how ladies should be spoken to. And now the Devil himself leads me into that cursed apple-basket, and now I must sit moping in solitude, with nothing but a poor pipe of-"

Here the Student Anselmus was interrupted in his soliloquy by a strange rustling and whisking, which rose close by him in the grass, but soon glided up into the twigs and leaves of the elder-tree that stretched out over his head. It was as if the evening wind were shaking the leaves, as if little birds were twittering among the branches, moving their little wings in capricious flutter to and fro. Then he heard a whispering and lisping, and it seemed as if the blossoms were sounding like little crystal bells. Anselmus listened and listened. Ere long, the whispering, and lisping, and tinkling, he himself knew not how, grew to faint and half-scattered words:

"'Twixt this way, 'twixt that; 'twixt branches, 'twixt blossoms, come shoot, come twist and twirl we! Sisterkin, sisterkin! up to the shine; up, down, through and through, quick! Sunrays yellow; evening wind whispering; dewdrops pattering; blossoms all singing: sing we with branches and blossoms! Stars soon glitter; must down: 'twixt this way, 'twixt that, come shoot, come twist, come twirl we, sisterkin!"

And so it went along, in confused and confusing speech. The Student Anselmus thought:

"Well, it is only the evening wind, which tonight truly is whispering distinctly enough." But at that moment there sounded over his head, as it were, a triple harmony of clear crystal bells: he looked up, and perceived three little snakes, glittering with green and gold, twisted around the branches, and stretching out their heads to the evening sun. Then, again, began a whispering and twittering in the same words as before, and the little snakes went gliding and caressing up and down through the twigs; and while they moved so rapidly, it was as if the elder-bush were scattering a thousand glittering emeralds through the dark leaves.

"It is the evening sun sporting in the elder-bush," thought the Student Anselmus; but the bells sounded again; and Anselmus observed that one snake held out its little head to him. Through all his limbs there went a shock like electricity; he quivered in his inmost heart: he kept gazing up, and a pair of glorious dark-blue eyes were looking at him with unspeakable longing; and an unknown feeling of highest blessedness and deepest sorrow nearly rent his heart asunder. And as he looked, and still looked, full of warm desire, into those kind eyes, the crystal bells sounded louder in harmonious accord, and the glittering emeralds fell down and encircled him, flickering round him in a thousand sparkles and sporting in resplendent threads of gold. The elder-bush moved and spoke: "You lay in my shadow; my perfume flowed around you, but you understood it not. The perfume is my speech, when love kindles it." The evening wind came gliding past, and said: "I played round your temples, but you understood me not. That breath is my speech, when love kindles it." The sunbeam broke through the clouds, and the sheen of it burned, as in words: "I overflowed you, with glowing gold, but you understood me not. That glow is my speech, when love kindles it."

And, still deeper and deeper sank in the view of those glorious eyes, his longing grew keener, his desire more warm. And all rose and moved around him, as if awakening to glad life. Flowers and blossoms shed their odours round him, and their odour was like the lordly singing of a thousand softest voices, and what they sang was borne, like an echo, on the golden evening clouds, as they flitted away, into far-off lands. But as the last sunbeam abruptly sank behind the hills, and the twilight threw its veil over the scene, there came a hoarse deep voice, as from a great distance:

"Hey! hey! what chattering and jingling is that up there? Hey! hey! who catches me the ray behind the hills? Sunned enough, sung enough. Hey! hey! through bush and grass, through grass and stream. Hey! hey! Come dow-w-n, dow-w-w-n!". So the voice faded away, as in murmurs of a distant thunder; but the crystal bells broke off in sharp discords. All became mute; and the Student Anselmus observed how the three snakes, glittering and sparkling, glided through the grass towards the river; rustling and hustling, they rushed into the Elbe; and over the waves where they vanished, there crackled up a green flame, which, gleaming forward obliquely, vanished in the direction of the city.

14

Second Vigil

"**The** gentleman is ill?" said a decent burgher's wife, who returning from a walk with her family, had paused here, and, with crossed arms, was looking at the mad pranks of the Student Anselmus. Anselmus had clasped the trunk of the elder-tree, and was calling incessantly up to the branches and leaves: "O glitter and shine once more, dear gold snakes: let me hear your little bell-voices once more! Look on me once more, kind eyes; O once, or I must die in pain and warm longing!" And with this, he was sighing and sobbing from the bottom of his heart most pitiftilly; and in his eagerness and impatience, shaking the elder-tree to and fro; which, however, instead of any reply, rustled quite stupidly and unintelligibly with its leaves; and so rather seemed, as it were, to make sport of the Student Anselmus and his sorrows.

"The gentleman is ill!" said the burgher's wife; and Anselmus felt as if someone had shaken him out of a deep dream, or poured ice-cold water on him, to awaken him without loss of time.

He now first saw clearly where he was, and recollected what a strange apparition had assaulted him, nay, so beguiled his senses, as to make him break forth into loud talk with himself. In astonishment, he gazed at the woman, and at last snatching up his hat, which had fallen to the ground in his transport, was about to make off in all speed. The burgher himself had come toward in the meanwhile, and, setting down the child from his arm on the grass, had been leaning

15

on his staff, and with amazement listening and looking at the Student. He now picked up the pipe and tobacco-box which the Student had let fall, and, holding them out to him, said: "Don't take on so dreadfully, my worthy sir, or alarm people in the dark, when nothing is the matter, after all, but a drop or two of christian liquor: go home, like a good fellow, and sleep it off."

The Student Anselmus felt exceedingly ashamed; he uttered nothing but a most lamentable Ah!

"Pooh! Pooh!" said the burgher, "never mind it a jot; such a thing will happen to the best; on good old Ascension Day a man may readily enough forget himself in his joy, and gulp down a thought too much. A clergyman himself is no worse for it: I presume, my worthy sir, you are a Candidatus. But, with your leave, sir, I shall fill my pipe with your tobacco; mine was used up a little while ago."

This last sentence the burgher uttered while the Student Anselmus was about to put away his pipe and box; and now the burgher slowly and deliberately cleaned his pipe, and began as slowly to fill it. Several burgher girls had come up: these were speaking secretly with the woman and each other, and tittering as they looked at Anselmus. The Student felt as if he were standing on prickly thorns, and burning needles. No sooner had he got back his pipe and tobacco-box, than he darted off as fast as he could.

All the strange things he had seen were clean gone from his memory; he simply recollected having babbled all sorts of foolish stuff beneath the elder-tree. This was the more frightful to him, as he entertained an inward horror against all soliloquists. It is Satan that chatters out of them, said his Rector; and Anselmus had honestly believed him. But to be regarded as a Candidatus Theologiee, overtaken with drink on Ascension Day! The thought was intolerable..Running on with these mad vexations, he was just about turning up Poplar Alley, by the Kosel garden, when a voice behind him called out: "Herr Anselmus! Herr Anselmus! for the love of Heaven, where are you running in such a hurry?" The Student paused, as if rooted to the ground; for he was convinced that now some new accident would befall him. The voice rose again: "Herr Anselmus, come back: we are waiting for you here at the water!" And now the Student perceived that it was his friend Conrector Paulmann's voice: he went back to the Elbe, and found the Conrector, with his two daughters, as well as Registrator Heerbrand, all about to step into their gondola. Conrector Paulmann invited the Student to go with them across the Elbe, and then to pass the evening at his house in the suburb of Pirna. The Student Anselmus very gladly accepted this proposal, thinking thereby to escape the malignant destiny which had ruled over him all day.

Now, as they were crossing the river, it chanced that on the farther bank in Anton's Garden, some fireworks were just going off. Sputtering and hissing, the rockets went aloft, and their blazing stars flew to pieces in the air, scattering a thousand vague shoots and flashes around them. The Student Anselmus was sitting by the steersman, sunk in deep thought, but when he noticed in the water the reflection of these darting and wavering sparks and flames, he felt as if it were the little golden snakes that were sporting in the flood. All the wonders that he had seen at the elder-tree again started forth into his heart and thoughts; and again that unspeakable longing, that glowing desire, laid hold of him here, which had agitated his bosom before in painful spasms of rapture.

"Ah! is it you again, my little golden snakes? Sing now, O sing! In your song let the kind, dear, dark-blue eyes again appear to me-Ah! are you under the waves, then?"

So cried the Student Anselmus, and at the same time made a violent movement, as if he was about to plunge into the river.

"Is the Devil in you, sir?" exclaimed the steersman, and clutched him by the lapels. The girls, who were sitting by him, shrieked in terror, and fled to the other side of the gondola. Registrator Heerbrand whispered something in Conrector Paulmann's ear, to which the latter answered at considerable length, but in so low a tone that Anselmus could distinguish nothing but the words:

"Such attacks more than once?-Never heard of it." Directly after this, Conrector Paulmann also rose, and then sat down, with a certain earnest, grave, official mien beside the Student Anselmus, taking his hand and saying: "How are you, Herr Anselmus?"

The Student Anselmus was almost losing his wits, for in his mind there was a mad contradiction, which he strove in vain to reconcile. He now saw plainly that what he had taken for the gleaming of the golden snakes was nothing but the reflection of the fireworks in Anton's Garden: but a feeling unexperienced till now, he himself did not know whether it was rapture or pain, cramped his breast together; and when the steersman struck through the water with his helm, so that the waves, curling as in anger, gurgled and chafed, he heard in their din a soft whispering: "Anselmus! Anselmus! do you see how we still skim along before you? Sisterkin looks at you again: believe, believe, believe in us!" And he thought he saw in the reflected light three green-glowing streaks: but then, when he gazed, full of fond sadness, into the water, to see whether those gentle eyes would not look up to him again, he perceived too well that the shine proceeded only from the windows in the neighbouring houses. He was sitting mute in his place, and inwardly battling with himself, when Conrector Paulmann repeated, with still greater emphasis: "How are you, Herr Anselmus?"

With the most rueful tone, Anselmus replied: "Ah! Herr Conrector, if you knew what strange things I have been dreaming, quite awake, with open eyes, just now, under an elder-tree at the wall of Linke's Garden, you would not take it amiss of me that I am a little absent, or so." "Ey, ey, Herr Anselmus!" interrupted Conrector Paulmann, "I have always taken you for a solid young man: but to dream, to dream with your eyes wide open, and then, all at once, to start up and try to jump into the water! This, begging your pardon, is what only fools or madmen would do."

The Student Anselmus was deeply affected by his friend's

hard saying; then Veronica, Paulniann's eldest daughter, a most pretty blooming girl of sixteen, addressed her father: "But, dear father, something singular must have befallen Herr Anselmus; and perhaps he only thinks he was awake, while he may have really been asleep, and so all manner of wild stuff has come into his head, and is still lying in his thoughts."

"And, dearest Mademoiselle! Worthy Conrector!" cried Registrator Heerbrand, "may one not, even when awake, sometimes sink into a sort of dream state? I myself have had such fits. One afternoon, for instance, during coffee, in a sort of brown study like this, in the special season of corporeal and spiritual digestion, the place where a lost Act was lying occurred to me, as if by inspiration; and last night, no farther gone, there came a glorious large Latin paper tripping out before my open eyes, in the very same way."

"Ah! most honoured Registrator," answered Conrector Paulmann, "you have always had a tendency to the Poetica; and thus one falls into fantasies and romantic humours."

The Student Anselmus, however, was particularly gratified that in this most troublous situation, while in danger of being considered drunk or crazy, anyone should take his part; and though it was already pretty dark, he thought he noticed, for the first time, that Veronica had really very fine dark blue eyes, and this too without remembering the strange pair which he had looked at in the elder-bush. Actually, the adventure under the elder-bush had once more entirely vanished from the thoughts of the Student Anselmus; he felt himself at ease and light of heart; nay, in the capriciousness of joy, he carried it so far, that he offered a helping hand to his fair advocate Veronica, as she was stepping from the gondola; and without more ado, as she put her arm in his, escorted her home with so much dexterity and good luck that he only missed his footing once, and this being the only wet spot in the whole road, only spattered Veronica's white gown a very little by the incident.

Conrector Paulmann did not fail to observe this happy change in the Student Anselmus; he resumed his liking for him and begged forgiveness for the hard words which he had let fall before. "Yes," added he, "we have many examples to show that certain phantasms may rise before a man, and pester and plague him not a little; but this is bodily disease, and leeches are good for it, if applied to the right part, as a certain learned physician, now deceased, has directed." The Student Anselmus did not know whether he had been drunk, crazy, or sick; but in any case the leeches seemed entirely superfluous, as these supposed phantasms had utterly vanished, and the Student himself was growing happier and happier the more he prospered in serving the pretty Veronica with all sorts of dainty attentions.

As usual, after the frugal meal, there came music; the Student Anselmus had to take his seat before the harpsichord, and Veronica accompanied his playing with her pure clear voice: "Dear Mademoiselle," said Registrator Heerbrand, "you have a voice like a crystal bell!"

"That she has not!" ejaculated the Student Anselmus,

he scarcely knew how. "Crystal bells in elder-trees sound strangely! strangely!" continued the Student Anselmus, murmuring half aloud.

Veronica laid her hand on his shoulder, and asked: "What are you saying now, Herr Anselmus?"

Instantly Anselmus recovered his cheerfulness, and began playing. Conrector Paulmann gave him a grim look; but Registrator Heerbrand laid a music leaf on the rack, and sang with ravishing grace one of Bandmaster Graun's bravura airs. The Student Anselmus accompanied this, and much more; and a fantasy duet, which Veronica and he now fingered, and Conrector Paulmann had himself composed, again brought everyone into the gayest humour.

It was now pretty late, and Registrator Heerbrand was taking up his hat and stick, when Conrector Paulmann went up to him with a mysterious air, and said: "Hem! Would not you, honoured Registrator, mention to the good Herr Anselmus himself-Hem! what we were speaking of before?"

"With all the pleasure in the world," said Registrator Heerbrand, and having placed himself in the circle, began, without farther preamble, as follows:

"In this city is a strange remarkable man; people say he follows all manner of secret sciences."

But as there are no such sciences, I take him rather for an antiquary, and along with this for an experimental chemist. I mean no other than our Privy Archivarius Lindhorst. He lives, as you know, by himself, in his old isolated house; and when he is away from his office, he is to be found in his library or in his chemical laboratory, to which, however, he admits no stranger.

Besides many curious books, he possesses a number of manuscripts, partly Arabic, Coptic, and some of them in strange characters, which do not belong to any known tongue. These he wishes to have copied properly, and for this purpose he requires a man who can draw with the pen, and so transfer these marks to parchment, in Indian ink, with the highest exactness and fidelity. The work is to be carried on in a separate chamber of his house, under his own supervision; and besides free board during the time of business, he will pay his copyist a speziesthaler, or specie-dollar, daily, and promises a handsome present when the copying is rightly finished. The hours of work are from twelve to six. From three to four, you take rest and dinner.

"Herr Archivarius Lindhorst having in vain tried one or two young people for copying these manuscripts, has at last applied to me to find him an expert calligrapher, and so I have been thinking of you, my dear Anselmus, for I know that you both write very neatly and draw with the pen to great perfection. Now, if in these bad times, and till your future establishment, you would like to earn a speziesthaler every day, and a present over and above your salary, you can go tomorrow precisely at noon, and call upon the Archivarius, whose house no doubt you know. But be on your guard against blots! If such a thing falls on your copy, you must begin it again; if it falls on the original, the Archivarius will think nothing of throwing you out the window, for he is a hot-tempered man."

The Student Anselmus was filled with joy at Registrator Heerbrand's proposal; for not only could the Student write well and draw well with the pen, but this copying with laborious calligraphic pains was a thing he delighted in more than anything else. So he thanked his patron in the most grateful terms, and promised not to fail at noon tomorrow.

All night the Student Anselmus saw nothing but clear speziesthalers, and heard nothing but their lovely clink. Who could blame the poor youth, cheated of so many hopes by capricious destiny, obliged to take counsel about every farthing, and to forego so many joys which a young heart requires! Early in the morning he brought out his black-lead pencils, his crowquills, his Indian ink; for better materials, thought he, the Archivarius can find nowhere. Above all, he gathered together and arranged his calligraphic masterpieces and his drawings, to show them to the Archivarius, as proof of his ability to do what was desired. Everything went well with the Student; a peculiar happy star seemed to be presiding over him; his neckcloth sat right at the very first trial; no stitches burst; no loop gave way in his black silk stockings; his hat did not once fall to the dust after he had trimmed it. In a word, precisely at half-past eleven, the Student Anselmus, in his pike-gray frock and black satin lower habiliments, with a roll of calligraphic specimens and pendrawings in his pocket, was standing in the Schlossgasse, or Castle Alley, in Conradi's shop, and drinking one-two glasses of the best stomachic liqueur; for here, thought he, slapping his pocket, which was still empty, for here speziesthalers will soon be chinking.

Notwithstanding the distance of the solitary street where the Archivarius Lindhorst's ancient residence lay, the Student Anselmus was at the front door before the stroke of twelve. He stood there, and was looking at the large fine bronze knocker; but now when, as the last stroke tingled through the air with a loud clang from the steeple clock of the Kreuzkirche, or Church of the Cross, he lifted his hand to grasp this same knocker, the metal visage twisted itself with a horrid rolling of its blue-gleaming eyes, into a grinning smile. Alas, it was the Applewoman of the Schwarzthor! The pointed teeth gnashed together in the loose jaws, and in their chattering through the skinny lips, there was a growl as of "You fool, fool, fool!-Wait, wait!-Why did you run!-Fool!" Horror-struck, the Student Anselmus flew back; he clutched at the door-post, but his hand caught the bell-rope, and pulled it, and in piercing discords it rang stronger and stronger, and through the whole empty house the echo repeated, as in mockery: "To the crystal, fall!" An unearthly terror seized the Student Anselmus, and quivered through all his limbs. The bell-rope lengthened downwards, and became a gigantic, transparent, white serpent, which encircled and crushed him, and girded him straiter and straiter in its coils, till his brittle paralyzed limbs went crashing in pieces and the blood spouted from his veins, penetrating into the transparent body of the serpent and dyeing it red. "Kill me! Kill me!" he wanted to cry, in his horrible agony; but the cry was only a stifled gurgle in his throat. The serpent lifted

25

its head, and laid its long peaked tongue of glowing brass on the breast of Anselmus; then a fierce pang suddenly cut asunder the artery of life, and thought fled away from him. On returning to his senses, he was lying on his own poor truckle-bed; Conrector Paulmann was standing before him, and saying: "For Heaven's sake, what mad stuff is this, dear Herr Anselmus?"

Third Vigil

"The Spirit looked upon the water, and the water moved itself and chafed in foaming billows, and plunged thundering down into the abysses, which opened their black throats and greedily swallowed it. Like triumphant conquerors, the granite rocks lifted their cleft peaky crowns, protecting the valley, till the sun took it into his paternal bosom, and clasping it with his beams as with glowing arms, cherished it and warmed it. Then a thousand germs, which had been sleeping under the desert sand, awoke from their deep slumber, and stretched out their little leaves and stalks towards the sun their father's face; and like smiling infants in green cradles, the flowrets rested in their buds and blossoms, till they too, awakened by their father, decked themselves in lights, which their father, to please them, tinted in a thousand varied hues.

"But in the midst of the valley was a black hill, which heaved up and down like the breast of man when warm longing swells it. From the abysses mounted steaming vapours, which rolled themselves together into huge masses, striving malignantly to hide the father's face: but he called the storm to him, which rushed there, and scattered them away; and when the pure sunbeam rested again on the bleak hill, there started from it, in the excess of its rapture, a glorious Fire-lily, opening its fair leaves like gentle lips to receive the kiss of its father.

"And now came a gleaming splendour into the valley; it was the youth Phosphorus; the Lily saw him, and begged,

27

being seized with warm longing love: 'Be mine for ever, fair youth! For I love you, and must die if you forsake me!' Then spoke the youth Phosphorus: 'I will be yours, fair flower; but then, like a naughty child, you will leave father and mother; you will know your playmates no longer, will strive to be greater and stronger than all that now rejoices with you as your equal. The longing which now beneficently warms your whole being will be scattered into a thousand rays and torture and vex you, for sense will bring forth senses; and the highest rapture, which the spark I cast into you kindles, will be the hopeless pain wherein you shall perish, to spring up anew in foreign shape. This spark is thought!'

"'Ah!' mourned the Lily, 'can I not be yours in this glow, as it now burns in me; not still be yours? Can I love you more than now; could I look on you as now, if you were to annihilate me?' Then the youth Phosphorus kissed the Lily; and as if penetrated with light, it mounted up in flame, out of which issued a foreign being, that hastily flying from the valley, roved forth into endless space, no longer heeding its old playmates, or the youth it had loved. This youth mourned for his lost beloved; for he too loved her, it was love to the fair Lily that had brought him to the lone valley; and the granite rocks bent down their heads in participation of his grief.

"But one of these opened its bosom, and there came a black-winged dragon flying out of it, who said: 'My brethren, the Metals are sleeping in there; but I am always brisk and waking, and will help you.' Dashing forth on its black pinions, the dragon at last caught the being which had sprung from the Lily; bore it to the hill, and encircled it with his wing; then was it the Lily again; but thought, which continued with it, tore asunder its heart; and its love for the youth Phosphorus was a cutting pain, before which, as if breathed on by poisonous vapours, the flowrets which had once rejoiced in the fair Lily's presence, faded and died.

"The youth Phosphorus put on a glittering coat of mail, sporting with the light in a thousand hues, and did battle with the dragon, who struck the cuirass with his black wing, till it rung and sounded; and at this loud clang the flowrets again came to life, and like variegated birds fluttered round the dragon, whose force departed; and who, thus being vanquished, hid himself in the depths of the earth. The Lily was freed; the youth Phosphorus clasped her, full of warm longing, of heavenly love; and in triumphant chorus, the flowers, the birds, nay, even the high granite rocks, did reverence to her as the Queen of the Valley."

"By your leave, worthy Herr Archivarius, this is Oriental bombast," said Registrator Heerbrand: "and we beg very much you would rather, as you often do, give us something of your own most remarkable life, of your travelling adventures, for instance; above all, something true."

"What the deuce, then?" answered Archivarius Lindhorst. "True? This very thing I have been telling is the truest I could dish out for you, my friends, and belongs to my life too, in a certain sense. For I come from that very valley; and the Fire-lily, which at last ruled as queen there, was my great-great-great-great-grandmother; and so, properly speaking,

I am a prince myself." All burst into a peal of laughter. "Ay, laugh your fill," continued Archivarius Lindhorst. "To you this matter, which I have related, certainly in the most brief and meagre way, may seem senseless and mad; yet, notwithstanding this, it is meant for anything but incoherent, or even allegorical, and it is, in one word, literally true. Had I known, however, that the glorious love story, to which I owe my existence, would have pleased you so little, I might have given you a little of the news my brother brought me on his visit yesterday."

"What, what is this? Have you a brother, then, Herr Archivarius? Where is he? Where does he live? In his Majesty's service too? Or perhaps a private scholar?" cried the company from all quarters.

"No!" replied the Archivarius, quite cool, composedly taking a pinch of snuff, "he has joined the bad side; he has gone over to the Dragons." "What do you mean, dear Herr Archivarius?" cried Registrator Heerbrand: "Over to the Dragons?"-"Over to the Dragons?" resounded like an echo from all hands.

"Yes, over to the Dragons," continued Archivarius Lindhorst: "it was sheer desperation, I believe. You know, gentlemen, my father died a short while ago; it is but three hundred and eighty-five years ago at most, and I am still in mourning for it. He had left me, his favourite son, a fine onyx; this onyx, rightly or wrongly, my brother would have: we quarrelled about it, over my father's corpse; in such unseemly manner that the good man started up, out of all patience, and threw my wicked brother downstairs. This stuck in our brother's stomach, and so without loss of time he went over to the Dragons. At present, he lives in a cypress wood, not far from Tunis: he has a famous magical carbuncle to watch there, which a dog of necromancer, who has set up a summerhouse in Lapland, has an eye to; so my poor brother only gets away for a quarter of an hour or so, when the necromancer happens to be out looking after the salamander bed in his garden, and then he tells me in all haste what good news there is about the Springs of the Nile."

For the second time, the company burst out into a peal of laughter: but the Student Anselmus began to feel quite dreary in heart; and he could scarcely look in Archivarius Lindhorst's parched countenance, and fixed earnest eyes, without shuddering internally in a way which he could not himself understand. Moreover, in the harsh and strangely metallic sound of Archivarius Lindhorst's voice there was something mysteriously piercing for the Student Anselmus, and he felt his very bones and marrow tingling as the Archivarius spoke.

The special object for which Registrator Heerbrand had taken him into the coffee house, seemed at present not attainable. After that accident at Archivarius Lindhorst's door, the Student Anselmus had withstood all inducements to risk a second visit: for, according to his own heart-felt conviction, it was only chance that had saved him, if not from death, at least from the danger of insanity. Conrector Paulmann had happened to be passing through the street at the time when

Anselmus was lying quite senseless at the door, and an old woman, who had laid her cookie-and-apple basket aside, was busied about him. Conrector Paulmann had forthwith called a chair, and so had him carried home. "Think what you will of me," said the Student Anselmus, "consider me a fool or not: I say, the cursed visage of that witch at the Schwarzthor grinned on me from the doorknocker. What happened after I would rather not speak of: but if I had recovered from my faint and seen that infernal Apple-wife beside me (for the old woman whom you talk of was no other), I should that instant have been struck by apoplexy, or have run stark mad."

All persuasions, all sensible arguments on the part of Conrector Paulmann and Registrator Heerbrand, profited nothing; and even the blue-eyed Veronica herself could not raise him from a certain moody humour, in which he had ever since been sunk. In fact, these friends regarded him as troubled in mind, and considered ways for diverting his thoughts; to which end, Registrator Heerbrand thought, there could nothing be so serviceable as copying Archivarius Lindhorst's manuscripts. The business, therefore, was to introduce the Student in some proper way to Archivarius Lindhorst; and so Registrator Heerbrand, knowing that the Archivarius used to visit a certain coffee house almost nightly, had invited the Student Anselmus to come every evening to that same coffee house, and drink a glass of beer and smoke a pipe, at his, the Registrator's charge, till such time as Archivarius Lindhorst should in one way or another see him, and the bargain for this copying work be settled; which offer the Student Anselmus had most gratefully accepted. "God will reward you, worthy Registrator, if you bring the young man to reason!" said Conrector Paulmann. "God will reward you!" repeated Veronica, piously raising her eyes to heaven, and vividly thinking that the Student Anselmus was already a most pretty young man, even without any reason.. Now accordingly, as Archivarius Lindhorst, with hat and staff, was making for the door, Registrator Heerbrand seized the Student Anselmus briskly by the hand, and stepping to meet the Herr Archivarius, he said: "Most esteemed Herr Archivarius, here is the Student Anselmus, who has an uncommon talent in calligraphy and drawing, and will undertake the copying of your rare manuscripts."

"I am most particularly glad to hear it," answered Archivarius Lindhorst sharply, then threw his three-cocked military hat on his head, and shoving Registrator Heerbrand and the Student Anselmus aside, rushed downstairs with great tumult, so that both of them were left standing in great confusion, gaping at the door, which he had slammed in their faces till the bolts and hinges of it rung again.

"He is a very strange old gentleman," said Registrator Heerbrand. "Strange old gentleman. "

stammered the Student Anselmus, with a feeling as if an ice-stream were creeping over all his veins, and he were stiffening into a statue. All the guests, however, laughed, and said: "Our Archivarius is on his high horse today: tomorrow, you shall see, he will be mild as a lamb again, and won't speak a word, but will look into the smoke-vortexes of his pipe, or read the newspapers; you must not mind these freaks."

"That is true too," thought the Student Anselmus: "who would mind such a thing, after all? Did not the Archivarius tell me he was most particularly glad to hear that I would undertake the copying of his manuscripts; and why did Registrator Heerbrand step directly in his way, when he was going home? No, no, he is a good man at bottom this Privy Archivarius Lindhorst, and sur-prisingly liberal. A little curious in his figures of speech; but what is that to me? Tomorrow at the stroke of twelve I will go to him, though fifty bronze Apple-wives should try to hinder me!"

Fourth Vigil

Gracious reader, may I venture to ask you a question? Have you ever had hours, perhaps even days or weeks, in which all your customary activities did nothing but cause you vexation and dis-satisfaction; when everything that you usually consider worthy and important seemed trivial and worthless? At such a time you did not know what to do or where to turn. A dim feeling pervaded your breast that you had higher desires that must be fulfilled, desires that transcended the pleasures of this world, yet desires which your spirit, like a cowed child, did not even dare to utter. In this longing for an unknown Something, which longing hovered above you no matter where you were, like an airy dream with thin transparent forms that melted away each time you tried to examine them, you had no voice for the world about you. You passed to and fro with troubled look, like a hopeless lover, and no matter what you saw being attempted or attained in the bustle of varied existence, it awakened no sorrow or joy in you. It was as if you had no share in this sublunary world.

If, favourable reader, you have ever been in this mood, you know the state into which the Student Anselmus had fallen. I wish most heartily, courteous reader, that it were in my power to bring the Student Anselmus before your eyes with true vividness. For in these vigils in which I record his singular history, there is still so much more of the marvellous-which is likely to make the everyday life of ordinary mortals seem pallid-that I fear in the end you will believe in neither the Student Anselmus nor Archivarius Lindhorst; indeed, that you will even entertain doubts as to Registrator Heerbrand and Conrector Paulmann, though these two estimable persons, at least, are still walking the pavements of Dresden. Favourable reader, while you are in the faery region of glorious wonders, where both rapture and horror may be evoked; where the goddess of earnestness herself will waft her veil aside and show her countenance (though a smile often glimmers in her glance, a sportive teasing before perplexing enchantments, comparable to mothers nursing and dandling their children)-while you are in this region which the spirit lays open to us in dreams, make an effort to recognize the well-known forms which hover around you in fitful brightness even in ordinary life. You will then find that this glorious kingdom lies much closer at hand than you ever supposed; it is this kingdom which I now very heartily desire, and am striving to show you in the singular story of the Student Anselmus.

So, as was hinted, the Student Anselmus, ever since that evening when he met with Archivarius Lindhorst, had been sunk in a dreamy musing, which rendered him insensible to every outward touch from common life. He felt that an unknown Something was awakening his inmost soul, and calling forth that rapturous pain, which is even the mood of longing that announces a loftier existence to man. He delighted most when he could rove alone through meads and woods; and as if released from all that fettered him to his necessary life, could, so to speak, again find himself in the manifold images which mounted from his soul.

It happened once that in returning from a long ramble, he passed by that notable elder-tree, under which, as if taken with faery, he had formerly beheld so many marvels. He felt himself strangely attracted by the green kindly sward; but no sooner had he seated himself on it than the whole vision which he had previously seen as in a heavenly trance, and which had since as if by foreign influence been driven from his mind, again came floating before him in the liveliest colours, as if he had been looking on it a second time. Nay, it was clearer to him now than ever, that the gentle blue eyes belonged to the gold-green snake, which had wound itself through the middle of the elder-tree; and that from the turnings of its tapering body all those glorious crystal tones, which had filled him with rapture, must have broken forth. As on Ascension Day, he again clasped the elder-tree to his bosom, and cried into the twigs and leaves: "Ah, once more shoot forth, and turn and wind yourself among the twigs, little fair green snake, that I may see you!"

"Once more look at me with your gentle eyes! Ab, I love you, and must die in pain and grief, if you do not return!" All, however, remained quite dumb and still; and as before, the elder-tree rustled quite unintelligibly with its twigs and leaves. But the Student Anselmus now felt as if he knew what it was that so moved and worked within him, nay, that so tore his bosom in the pain of an infinite longing. "What else is it," said he, "but that I love you with my whole heart and soul, and even to the death, glorious little golden snake; nay, that without you I cannot live, and must perish in hopeless woe, unless I find you again, unless I have you as the beloved of my heart. But I know it, you shall be mine; and then all that glorious dreams have promised me of another higher world shall be fulfilled."

Henceforth the Student Anselmus, every evening, when the sun was scattering its bright gold over the peaks of the trees, was to be seen under the elder-bush, calling from the depths of his heart in most lamentable tones into the branches and leaves for a sight of his beloved, of his little gold-green snake. Once as he was going on with this, there suddenly stood before him a tall lean man, wrapped up in a wide light-gray surtout, who, looking at him with large fiery eyes, exclaimed: "Hey, hey, what whining and whimpering is this? Hey, hey, this is Herr Anselmus that was to copy my manuscripts." The Student Anselmus felt not a little terrified at hearing this voice, for it was the very same which on Ascension Day had called: "Hey, hey, what chattering and jingling is this," and so forth. For fright and astonishment, he could not utter a word. "What ails you, Herr Anselmus," continued Archivarius Lindhorst, for the stranger was no one else; "what do you want with the elder-tree, and why did you not come to me and set about your work?"

In fact, the Student Anselmus had never yet prevailed upon himself to visit Archivarius Lindhorst's house a second time, though, that evening, he had firmly resolved on doing it. But now at this moment, when he saw his fair dreams torn asunder, and that too by the same hostile voice which had once before snatched away his beloved, a sort of desperation came over him, and he broke out fiercely into these words: "You may think me mad or not, Herr Archivarius; it is all the same to me: but here in this bush, on Ascension Day, I saw the gold-green snake-ah! the beloved of my soul; and she spoke to me in glorious crystal tones; and you, you, Herr Archivarius, cried and shouted horribly over the water."

"How is this, my dear sir?" interrupted Archivarius Lindhorst, smiling quite inexpressibly, and taking snuff.

The Student Anselmus felt his breast becoming easy, now that he had succeeded in beginning this strange story; and it seemed to him as if he were quite right in laying the whole blame upon the Archivarius, and that it was he, and no one else, who had thundered so from the distance. He courageously proceeded: "Well, then, I will tell you the whole mystery that happened to me on Ascension evening; and then you may say and do, and think of me whatever you please." He accordingly disclosed the whole miraculous adventure, from his luckless upsetting of the apple basket, till the departure of the three gold-green snakes over the river; and how the people after that had thought him drunk or crazy. "All this," ended the Student Anselmus, "I actually saw with my eyes; and deep in my bosom those dear voices, which spoke to me, are still sounding in clear echo: it was in no way a dream; and if I am not to die of longing and desire, I must believe in these gold-green snakes, though I see by your smile, Herr Archivarius, that you hold these same snakes as nothing more than creatures of my heated and overstrained imagination."

"Not at all," replied the Archivarius, with the greatest calmness and composure; "the gold-green snakes, which you saw in the elder-bush, Herr Anselmus, were simply my three daughters; and that you have fallen over head and ears in love with the blue eyes of Serpentina the youngest, is now clear enough. Indeed, I knew it on Ascension Day myself: and as (on that occasion, sitting busied with my writing at home) I began to get annoyed with so much chattering and jingling, I called to the idle minxes that it was time to get home, for the sun was setting, and they had sung and basked enough."

The Student Anselmus felt as if he now merely heard in plain words something he had long dreamed of, and though he fancied he observed that elder-bush, wall and sward, and all objects about him were beginning slowly to whirl around, he took heart, and was ready to speak; but the Archivarius prevented him; for sharply pulling the glove from his left hand, and holding the stone of a ring, glittering in strange sparkles and flames before the Student's eyes, he said: "Look here, Herr Anselmus; what you see may do you good."

The Student Anselmus looked in, and O wonder! the stone emitted a cluster of rays; and the rays wove themselves together into a clear gleaming crystal mirror; in which, with many windings, now flying asunder, now twisted together, the three gold-green snakes were dancing and bounding. And when their tapering forms, glittering with a thousand sparkles, touched each other, there issued from them glorious tones, as of crystal bells; and the midmost of the three stretched forth her little head from the mirror, as if full of longing and desire, and her dark-blue eyes said: "Do you know me, then? Do you believe in me, Anselmus? In belief alone is love: can you love?" "O Serpentina! Serpentina!" cried the Student Anselmus in mad rapture; but Archivarius Lindhorst suddenly breathed on the mirror, and with an electric sputter the rays sank back into their focus; and on his hand there was now nothing but a little emerald, over which the Archivarius drew his glove.

"Did you see the golden snakes, Herr Anselmus?" said the Archivarius.

"Ah, good heaven, yes!" replied the Student, "and the fair dear Serpentina."

"Hush!" continued Archivarius Lindhorst, "enough for now: for the rest, if you decide to work with me, you may see my daughter often enough; or rather I will grant you this real satisfaction: if you stick tightly and truly to your task, that is to say, copy every mark with the greatest clearness and correctness. But you have not come to me at all, Herr Anselmus, although Registrator Heerbrand promised I should see you immediately, and I have waited several days in vain."

Not until the mention of Registrator Heerbrand's name did the Student Anselmus again feel as if he was really standing with his two legs on the ground, and he was really the Student Anselmus, and the man talking to him really Archivarius Lindhorst. The tone of indifference, with which the latter spoke, in such rude contrast with the strange sights which like a genuine necromancer he had called forth, awakened a certain horror in the Student, which the piercing look of those fiery eyes, glowing from their bony sockets in the lean puckered visage, as from a leathern case, still farther aggravated: and the Student was again forcibly seized with the same unearthly feeling, which had before gained possession of him in the coffee house, when Archivarius Lindhorst had talked so wildly. With a great effort he retained his self-command, and as the Archivarius again asked, "Well, why did you not come?" the Student exerted his whole energies, and related to him what had happened at the street door.

"My dear Herr Anselmus," said the Archivarius, when the Student was finished; "dear Herr Anselmus, I know this Apple-wife of whom you speak; she is a vicious slut that plays all sorts of vile tricks on me; but that she has turned herself to bronze and taken the shape of a doorknocker, to deter pleasant visitors from calling, is indeed very bad, and truly not to be endured. Would you please, worthy Herr Anselmus, if you come tomorrow at noon and notice any more of this grinning and growling, just be so good as to let a drop or two of this liquor fall on her nose; it will put everything to rights immediately. And now, adieu, my dear Herr Anselmus! I must make haste, therefore I would not advise you to think of returning with me. Adieu, till we meet!--Tomorrow at noon!"

The Archivarius had given the Student Anselmus a little vial, with a gold-coloured fluid in it; and he walked rapidly off; so rapidly, that in the dusk, which had now come on, he seemed to be floating down to the valley rather than walking down to it. Already he was near the Kosel garden; the wind got within his wide greatcoat, and drove its breasts asunder; so that they fluttered in the air like a pair of large wings; and to the Student Anselmus, who was looking full of amazement at the course of the Archivarius, it seemed as if a large bird were spreading out its pinions for rapid flight. And now, while the Student kept gazing into the dusk, a white-gray kite wit h creaking cry soared up into the air; and he now saw clearly that the white flutter which he had thought to be the retiring Archivarius must have been this very kite, though he still could not understand where the Archivarius had vanished so abruptly.

"Perhaps he may have flown away in person, this Herr Archivarius Lindhorst," said the Student Anselmus to himself; "for I now see and feel clearly, that all these foreign shapes of a distant wondrous world, which I never saw before except in peculiarly remarkable dreams, have now come into my waking life, and are making their sport of me. But be this as it will! You live and glow in my breast, lovely, gentle Serpentina; you alone can still the infinite longing which rends my soul to pieces. Ah, when shall I see your kind eyes, dear, dear Serpentina!" cried the Student Anselmus aloud.

"That is a vile unchristian name!" murmured a bass voice beside him, which belonged to some promenader returning home. The Student Anselmus, reminded where he was, hastened off at a quick pace, thinking to himself: "Wouldn't it be a real misfortune now if Conrector Paulmann or

Registrator Heerbrand were to meet me?"-But neither of these gentlemen met him.

Fifth Vigil

"There is nothing in the world that can be done with this Anselmus," said Conrector Paulmann; "all my good advice, all my admonitions, are fruitless; he will apply himself to nothing; though he is a fine classical scholar too, and that is the foundation of everything."

But Registrator Heerbrand, with a sly, mysterious smile, replied: "Let Anselmus take his time, my dear Conrector! he is a strange subject, this Anselmus, but there is much in him: and when I say much, I mean a Privy Secretary, or even a Court Councillor, a Hofrath."

"Hof-" began Conrector Paulmann, in the deepest amazement; the word stuck in his throat.

"Hush! hush!" continued Registrator Heerbrand, "I know what I know. These two days he has been with Archivarius Lindhorst, copying manuscripts; and last night the Archivarius meets me at the coffee house, and says: 'You have sent me a proper man, good neighbour! There is stuff in him!' And now think of Archivarius Lindhorst's influence-Hush! hush! we will talk of it this time a year from now." And with these words the Registrator, his face still wrinkled into the same sly smile, went out of the room, leaving the Conrector speechless with astonishment and curiosity, and fixed, as if by enchantment, in his chair.

But on Veronica this dialogue had made a still deeper impression. "Did I not know all along," she thought, "that Herr Anselmus was a most clever and pretty young man, to whom something great would come? Were I but certain that he really liked me! But that night when we crossed the Elbe, did he not press my hand twice? Did he not look at me, in our duet, with such glances that pierced into my very heart? Yes, yes! he really likes me; and I-" Veronica gave herself up, as young maidens are wont, to sweet dreams of a gay future. She was Mrs. Hofrath, Frau Hofräthinn; she occupied a fine house in the Schlossgasse, or in the Neumarkt, or in the Moritzstrasse; her fashionable hat, her new Turkish shawl, became her admirably; she was breakfasting on the balcony in an elegant negligee, giving orders to her cook for the day: "And see, if you please, not to spoil that dish; it is the Hofrath's favourite." Then passing beaux glanced up, and she heard distinctly: "Well, she is a heavenly woman, that Hofräthinn; how prettily the lace cap suits her!" Mrs. Privy Councillor Ypsilon sends her servant to ask if it would please the Frau Hofräthinn to drive as far as the Linke Bath today? "Many compliments; extremely sorry, I am engaged to tea already with the Presidentinn Tz." Then comes the Hofrath Anselmus back from his office; he is dressed in the top of the mode: "Ten, I declare," cries he, making his gold watch repeat, and giving his young lady a kiss. "How are things, little wife?"

"Guess what I have here for you?" he continues in a teasing manner, and draws from his waistcoat pocket a pair of beautiful earrings, fashioned in the newest style, and puts them on in place of the old ones. "Ah! What pretty, dainty earrings!" cried Veronica aloud; and started up from her chair, throwing aside her work, to see those fair earrings with her own eyes in the glass..."What is this?" said Conrector Paulmann, roused by the noise from his deep study of Cicero de Officiis, and almost dropping the book from his hand; "are we taking fits, like Anselmus?" But at this moment, the Student Anselmus, who, contrary to his custom, had not been seen for several days, entered the room, to Veronica's astonishment and terror; for, in truth, he seemed altered in his whole bearing. With a certain precision, which was far from usual in him, he spoke of new tendencies of life which had become clear to his mind, of glorious prospects which were opening for him, but which many did not have the skill to discern. Conrector Paulmann, remembering Registrator Heerhrand's mysterious speech, was still more struck, and could scarcely utter a syllable, till the Student Anselmus, after letting fall some hints of urgent business at Archivarius Lindhorst's, and with elegant adroitness kissing Veronica's hand, was already down the stairs, off and away.

"This was the Hofrath," murmured Veronica to herself: "and he kissed my hand, without sliding on the floor, or treading on my foot, as he used to! He threw me the softest look too; yes, he really loves me!"

Veronica again gave way to her dreaming; yet now, it was as if a hostile shape were still coming forward among these lovely visions of her future household life as Frau Hofräthinn, and the shape were laughing in spiteful mockery, and saying: "This is all very stupid and trashy stuff, and lies to boot; for Anselmus will never, never, be Hofrath or your husband; he does not love you in the least, though you have blue eyes, and a fine figure, and a pretty hand." Then an ice-stream poured over Veronica's soul; and a deep sorrow swept away the delight with which, a little while ago, she had seen herself in the lace cap and fashionable earrings. Tears almost rushed into her eyes, and she said aloud: "Ah! it is too true; he does not love me in the least; and I shall never, never, be Frau Hofräthinn!"

"Romantic idiocy, romantic idiocy!" cried Conrector Paulmann; then snatched his hat and stick, and hastened indignantly from the house. "This was still wanting," sighed Veronica; and felt vexed at her little sister, a girl of twelve years, because she sat so unconcerned, and kept sewing at her frame, as if nothing had happened.

Meanwhile it was almost three o'clock; and now time to tidy up the apartment, and arrange the coffee table: for the Mademoiselles Oster had announced that they were coming. But from behind every workbox which Veronica lifted aside, behind the notebooks which she took away from the harpsichord, behind every cup, behind the coffeepot which she took from the cupboard, that shape peeped forth, like a little mandrake, and laughed in spiteful mockery, and snapped its little spider fingers, and cried: "He will not be your husband! he will not be your husband!" And then, when she threw everything away, and fled to the middle of the room, it peered out again, with long nose, in gigantic bulk, from behind the stove, and snarled and growled: "He will not be your husband!"

"Don't you hear anything, don't you see anything?" cried Veronica, shivering with fright, and not daring to touch anything in the room. Fränzchen rose, quite grave and quiet, from her embroidering frame, and said, "What ails you today, sister? You are just making a mess. I must help you, I see."

But at this time the visitors came tripping in in a lively manner, with brisk laughter; and the same moment, Veronica perceived that it was the stove handle which she had taken for a shape, and the creaking of the ill-shut stove door for those spiteful words. Yet, overcome with horror, she did not immediately recover her composure, and her excitement, which her paleness and agitated looks betrayed, was noticed by the Mademoiselles Oster. As they at once cut short their merry talk, and pressed her to tell them what, in Heaven's name, had happened, Veronica was obliged to admit that certain strange thoughts had come into her mind; and suddenly, in open day a dread of spectres, which she did not normally feel, had got the better of her. She described in such lively colours how a little gray mannikin, peeping out of all the corners of the room, had mocked and plagued her, that the Mademoiselles Oster began to look around with timid glances, and began to have all sorts of unearthly notions. But Fränzchen entered at this moment with the steaming coffeepot; and the three, taking thought again, laughed outright at their folly.

Angelica, the elder of the Osters, was engaged to an officer; the young man had joined the army; but his friends had been so long without news of him that there was too little doubt of his being dead, or at least grievously wounded. This had plunged Angelica into the deepest sorrow; but today she was merry, even to extravagance, a state of things which so much surprised Veronica that she could not but speak of it, and inquire the reason.

"Darling," said Angelica, "do you fancy that my Victor is out of heart and thoughts? It is because of him I am so happy. O Heaven! so happy, so blessed in my whole soul! For my Victor is well; in a little while he will be home, advanced to Rittmeister, and decorated with the honours which he has won. A deep but not dangerous wound, in his right arm, which he got from a sword cut by a French hussar, prevents him from writing; and rapid change of quarters, for he will not consent to leave his regiment, makes it impossible for him to send me tidings. But tonight he will be ordered home, until his wound is cured. Tomorrow he will set out for home; and just as he is stepping into the coach, he will learn of his promotion to Rittmeister."

"But, my dear Angelica," interrupted Veronica. "How do you know all this?"

"Do not laugh at me, my friend," continued Angelica; "and surely you will not laugh, for the little gray mannikin, to punish you, might peep out from behind the mirror there. I cannot lay aside my belief in certain mysterious things, since often enough in life they have come before my eyes, I might say, into my very hands. For example, I cannot consider it so strange and incredible as many others do, that there should be people gifted with a certain faculty of prophecy.

50

In the city, here, is an old woman, who possesses this gift to a high degree. She does not use cards, nor molten lead, nor coffee grounds, like ordinary fortune tellers, but after certain preparations, in which you yourself take a part, she takes a polished metallic mirror, and the strangest mixture of figures and forms, all intermingled rise up in it. She interprets these and answers your question. I was with her last night, and got those tidings of my Victor, which I have not doubted for a moment."

Angelica's narrative threw a spark into Veronica's soul, which instantly kindled with the thought of consulting this same old prophetess about Anselmus and her hopes. She learned that the crone was called Frau Rauerin, and lived in a remote street near the Seethor; that she was not to be seen except on Tuesdays, Thursdays, and Fridays, from seven o'clock in the evening, but then, indeed, through the whole night till sunrise; and that she preferred her customers to come alone. It was now Thursday, and Veronica determined, under pretext of accompanying the Osters home, to visit this old woman, and lay the case before her.

Accordingly, no sooner had her friends, who lived in the Neustadt, parted from her at the Elbe Bridge, than she hastened towards the Seethor; and before long, she had reached the remote narrow street described to her, and at the end of it saw the little red house in which Frau Rauerin was said to live. She could not rid herself of a certain dread, nay, of a certain horror, as she approached the door. At last she summoned resolution, in spite of inward terror, and made bold to pull the bell: the door opened, and she groped through the dark passage for the stair which led to the upper story, as Angelica had directed. "Does Frau Rauerin live here?" cried she into the empty lobby as no one appeared; but instead of an answer, there rose a long clear "Mew!" and a large black cat, with its back curved up, and whisking its tail to and fro in wavy coils, stepped on before her, with much gravity, to the door of the apartment, which, on a second mew, was opened.

"Ah, see! Are you here already, daughter? Come in, love; come in!" exclaimed an advancing figure, whose appearance rooted Veronica to the floor. A long lean woman, wrapped in black rags!-while she spoke, her peaked projecting chin wagged this way and that; her toothless mouth, overshadowed by a bony hawk-nose, twisted itself into a ghastly smile, and gleaming cat's-eyes flickered in sparkles through the large spectacles. From a party-coloured clout wrapped round her head, black wiry hair was sticking out; but what deformed her haggard visage to absolute horror, were two large burn marks which ran from the left cheek, over the nose.

Veronica's breathing stopped; and the scream, which was about to lighten her choked breast, became a deep sigh, as the witch's skeleton hand took hold of her, and led her into the chamber.

Here everything was awake and astir; nothing but din and tumult, and squeaking, and mewing, and croaking, and piping all at once, on every hand. The crone struck the table with her fist, and screamed: "Peace, ye vermin!" And the meer-cats, whimpering, clambered to the top of the high bed; and the little meer-swine all ran beneath the stove, and the raven fluttered up to the round mirror; and the black cat, as if the rebuke did not apply to him, kept sitting at his ease on the cushioned chair, to which he had leapt directly after entering.

So soon as the room became quiet, Veronica took heart; she felt less frightened than she had outside in the hall; nay, the crone herself did not seem so hideous. For the first time, she now looked round the room. All sorts of odious stuffed beasts hung down from the ceiling: strange unknown household implements were lying in confusion on the floor; and in the grate was a scanty blue fire, which only now and then sputtered up in yellow sparkles; and at every sputter, there came a rustling from above and monstrous bats, as if with human countenances in distorted laughter, went flitting to and fro; at times, too, the flame shot up, licking the sooty wall, and then there sounded cutting howling tones of woe, which shook Veronica with fear and horror. "With your leave, Mamsell!" said the crone, knitting her brows, and seizing a brush; with which, having dipped it in a copper skillet, she then besprinkled the grate. The fire went out; and as if filled with thick smoke, the room grew pitch-dark: but the crone, who had gone aside into a closet, soon returned with a lighted lamp; and now Veronica could see no beasts or implements in the apartment; it was a common meanly furnished room. The crone came up to her, and said with a creaking voice: "I know what you wish, little daughter: tush, you would have me tell you whether you shall wed Anselmus, when he is Hofrath."

Veronica stiffened with amazement and terror, but the crone continued: "You told me the whole of it at home, at your father's, when the coffeepot was standing before you: I was the coffeepot; didn't you know me? Daughterkin, hear me! Give up, give up this Anselmus; he is a nasty creature; he trod my little sons to pieces, my dear little sons, the Apples with the red cheeks, that glide away, when people have bought them, whisk! out of their pockets, and roll back into my basket. He trades with the Old One: it was but the day before yesterday, he poured that cursed Auripigment on my face, and I nearly went blind with it. You can see the burn marks yet. Daughterkin, give him up, give him up! He does not love you, for he loves the gold-green snake; he will never be Hofrath, for he has joined the salamanders, and he means to wed the green snake: give him up, give him up!"

Veronica, who had a firm, steadfast spirit of her own, and could conquer girlish terror, now drew back a step, and said, with a serious resolute tone: "Old woman! I heard of your gift of looking into the future; and wished, perhaps too curiously and thoughtlessly, to learn from you whether Anselmus, whom I love and value, could ever be mine. But if, instead of fulfilling my desire, you keep vexing me with your foolish unreasonable babble, you are doing wrong; for I have asked of you nothing but what you grant to others, as I well know. Since you are acquainted with my inmost thoughts apparently, it might perhaps have been an easy matter for you to unfold to me much that now pains and grieves my mind;

but after your silly slander of the good Anselmus, I do not care to talk further with you. Goodnight!"

Veronica started to leave hastily, but the crone, with tears and lamentation, fell upon her knees; and, holding the young lady by the gown, exclaimed: "Veronica! Veronica! have you forgotten old Liese? Your nurse who has so often carried you in her arms, and dandled you?"

Veronica could scarcely believe her eyes; for here, in truth, was her old nurse, defaced only by great age and by the two burns; old Liese, who had vanished from Conrector Paulmann's house some years ago, no one knew where. The crone, too, had quite another look now: instead of the ugly many-pieced clout, she had on a decent cap; instead of the black rags, a gay printed bedgown; she was neatly dressed, as of old. She rose from the floor, and taking Veronica in her arms, proceeded: "What I have just told you may seem very mad; but, unluckily, it is too true. Anselmus has done me much mischief, though it is not his own fault: he has fallen into Archivarius Lindhorst's hands, and the Old One means to marry him to his daughter. Archivarius Lindhorst is my deadliest enemy: I could tell you thousands of things about him, which, however, you would not understand, or at best be too much frightened at. He is the Wise Man, it seems; but I am the Wise Woman: let this stand for that! I see now that you love this Anselmus; and I will help you with all my strength, that so you may be happy, and wed him like a pretty bride, as you wish."

"But tell me, for Heaven's sake, Liese-" interrupted Veronica.

"Hush! child, hush!" cried the old woman, interrupting in her turn: "I know what you would say; I have become what I am, because it was to be so: I could do no other. Well, then! I know the means which will cure Anselmus of his frantic love for the green snake, and lead him, the prettiest Hofrath, into your arms; but you yourself must help."

"Tell me, Liese; I will do anything and everything, for I love Anselmus very much!" whispered Veronica, scarcely audibly.

"I know you," continued the crone, "for a courageous child: I could never frighten you to sleep with the Wauwau; for that instant, your eyes were open to what the Wauwau was like. You would go without a light into the darkest room; and many a time, with papa's powder-mantle, you terrified the neighbours' children. Well, then, if you are in earnest about conquering Archivarius Lindhorst and the green snake by my art; if you are in earnest about calling Anselmus Hofrath and husband; then, at the next Equinox, about eleven at night, glide from your father's house, and come here: I will go with you to the crossroads, which cut the fields hard by here: we shall take what is needed, and whatever wonders you may see shall do you no whit of harm. And now, love, goodnight: Papa is waiting for you at supper."

Veronica hastened away: she had the firmest purpose not to neglect the night of the Equinox; "for," thought she, "old Liese is right; Anselmus has become entangled in strange fetters; but I will free him from them, and call him mine forever; mine he is, and shall be, the Hofrath Anselmus."

56

Sixth Vigil

"It may be, after all," said the Student Anselmus to himself, "that the superfine strong stomachic liqueur, which I took somewhat freely in Monsieur Conradi's, might really be the cause of all these shocking phantasms, which tortured me so at Archivarius Lindhorst's door. Therefore, I will go quite sober today, and so bid defiance to whatever farther mischief may assail me." On this occasion, as before when equipping himself for his first call on Archivarius Lindhorst, the Student Anselmus put his pen-drawings, and calligraphic masterpieces, his bars of Indian ink, and his well-pointed crow-pens, into his pockets; and was just turning to go out, when his eye lighted on the vial with the yellow liquor, which he had received from Archivarius Lindhorst. All the strange adventures he had met again rose on his mind in glowing colours; and a nameless emotion of rapture and pain thrilled through his breast. Involuntarily he exclaimed, with a most piteous voice: "Ah, am not I going to the Archivarius solely for a sight of you, gentle lovely Serpentina!" At that moment, he felt as if Serpentina's love might be the prize of some laborious perilous task which he had to undertake; and as if this task were nothing else but the copying of the Lindhorst manuscripts. That at his very entrance into the house, or more properly, before his entrance, all sorts of mysterious things might happen, as before, was no more than he anticipated.

He thought no more of Conradi's strong drink, but hastily put the vial of liquor in his waistcoat pocket, that he

57

might act strictly by the Archivarius' directions, should the bronze Apple-woman again take it upon her to make faces at him.

And the hawk-nose actually did peak itself, the cat-eyes actually did glare from the knocker, as he raised his hand to it, at the stroke of twelve. But now, without farther ceremony, he dribbled his liquor into the pestilent visage; and it folded and moulded itself, that instant, down to a glittering bowl-round knocker. The door opened, the bells sounded beautifully over all the house:

"Klingling, youngling, in, in, spring, spring, klingling." In good heart he mounted the fine broad stair; and feasted on the odours of some strange perfume that was floating through the house. In doubt, he paused in the hall; for he did not know at which of these many fine doors he was to knock. But Archivarius Lindhorst, in a white damask nightgown, emerged and said: "Well, it is a real pleasure to me, Herr Anselmus, that you have kept your word at last. Come this way, if you please; I must take you straight into the laboratory." And with this he stepped rapidly through the hall, and opened a little side door, which led into a long passage. Anselmus walked on in high spirits, behind the Archivarius; they passed from this corridor into a hall, or rather into a lordly greenhouse: for on both sides, up to the ceiling, grew all sorts of rare wondrous flowers, indeed, great trees with strangely formed leaves and blossoms. A magic dazzling light shone over the whole, though you could not discover where it came from, for no window whatever was to be seen. As the Student Anselmus looked in through the bushes and trees, long avenues appeared to open into remote distance. In the deep shade of thick cypress groves lay glittering marble fountains, out of which rose wondrous figures, spouting crystal jets that fell with pattering spray into the gleaming lily-cups. Strange voices cooed and rustled through the wood of curious trees; and sweetest perfumes streamed up and down.

The Archivarius had vanished: and Anselmus saw nothing but a huge bush of glowing fire-lilies before him. Intoxicated with the sight and the fine odours of this fairy-garden, Anselmus stood fixed to the spot. Then began on all sides of him a giggling and laughing; and light little voices railed at him and mocked him: "Herr Studiosus! Herr Studiosus! how did you get in here?"

"Why have you dressed so bravely, Herr Anselmus? Will you chat with us for a minute and tell us how grandmamma sat down upon the egg, and young master got a stain on his Sunday waistcoat?-Can you play the new tune, now, which you learned from Daddy Cockadoodle, Herr Anselmus?-You look very fine in your glass periwig, and brown-paper boots." So cried and chattered and sniggered the little voices, out of every corner, indeed, close by the Student himself, who now observed that all sorts of multicoloured birds were fluttering above him, and jeering at him. At that moment, the bush of fire-lilies advanced towards him; and he perceived that it was Archivarius Lindhorst, whose flowered nightgown, glittering in red and yellow, had deceived his eyes.

59

"I beg your pardon, worthy Herr Anselmus," said the Archivarius, "for leaving you alone: I wished, in passing, to take a peep at my fine cactus, which is to blossom tonight. But how do you like my little house-garden?"

"Ah, Heaven! It is inconceivably beautiful, Herr Archivarius," replied the Student; "but these multicoloured birds have been bantering me a little."

"What chattering is this?" cried the Archivarius angrily into the bushes. Then a huge gray Parrot came fluttering out, and perched itself beside the Archivarius on a myrtle bough, and looking at him with an uncommon earnestness and gravity through a pair of spectacles that stuck on its hooked bill, it creaked out: "Don't take it amiss, Herr Archivarius; my wild boys have been a little free or so; but the Herr Studiosus has himself to blame in the matter, for-"

"Hush! hush!" interrupted Archivarius Lindhorst; "I know the varlets; but you must keep them in better discipline, my friend!--Now, come along, Herr Anselmus."

And the Archivarius again stepped forth through many a strangely decorated chamber, so that the Student Anselmus, in following him, could scarcely give a glance at all the glittering wondrous furniture and other unknown things with which all the rooms were filled. At last they entered a large apartment, where the Archivarius, casting his eyes aloft, stood still; and Anselmus got time to feast himself on the glorious sight, which the simple decoration of this hall afforded. Jutting from the azure-coloured walls rose gold-bronze trunks of high palm-trees, which wove their colossal leaves, glittering like bright emeralds, into a ceiling far up: in the middle of the chamber, and resting on three Egyptian lions, cast out of dark bronze, lay a porphyry plate; and on this stood a simple flower pot made of gold, from which, as soon as he beheld it, Anselmus could not turn away his eyes. It was as if, in a thousand gleaming reflections, all sorts of shapes were sporting on the bright polished gold: often he perceived his own form, with arms stretched out in longing-ah! beneath the elder-bush-and Serpentina was winding and shooting up and down, and again looking at him with her kind eyes. Anselmus was beside himself with frantic rapture.

"Serpentina! Serpentina!" he cried aloud; and Archivarius Lindhorst whirled round abruptly, and said: "What, Herr Anselmus? If I am not wrong, you were pleased to call for my daughter; she is in the other side of the house at present, and indeed taking her lesson on the harpsichord. Let us go along."

Anselmus, scarcely knowing what he did, followed his conductor; he saw or heard nothing more till Archivarius Lindhorst suddenly grasped his hand and said: "Here is the place!"

Anselmus awoke as from a dream and now perceived that he was in a high room lined on all sides with bookshelves, and nowise differing from a common library and study. In the middle stood a large writing table, with a stuffed armchair before it. "This," said Archivarius Lindhorst, "is your workroom for the present: whether you may work, some other time, in the blue library, where you so suddenly called out my daughter's name, I do not know yet. But now I would like to convince myself of your ability to execute this task appointed you, in the way I wish it and need it." The Student here gathered full courage; and not without internal self-complacence in the certainty of highly gratifying Archivarius Lindhorst, pulled out his drawings and specimens of penmanship from his pocket. But no sooner had the Archivarius cast his eye on the first leaf, a piece of writing in the finest English style, than he smiled very oddly and shook his head. These motions he repeated at every succeeding leaf, so that the Student Anselmus felt the blood mounting to his face, and at last, when the smile became quite sarcastic and contemptuous, he broke out in downright vexation: "The Herr Archivarius does not seem contented with my poor talents."

"My dear Herr Anselmus," said Archivarius Lindhorst, "you have indeed fine capacities for the art of calligraphy; but, in the meanwhile, it is clear enough, I must reckon more on your diligence and good-will, than on your attainments."

The Student Anselmus spoke at length of his often-acknowledged perfection in this art, of his fine Chinese ink, and most select crow-quills. But Archivarius Lindhorst handed him the English sheet, and said: "Be the judge yourself!" Anselmus felt as if struck by a thunderbolt, to see the way his handwriting looked: it was miserable, beyond measure. There was no rounding in the turns, no hair-stroke where it should be; no proportion between the capital and single letters; indeed, villainous schoolboy pot-hooks often spoiled the best lines. "And then," continued Archivarius Lindhorst, "your ink will not last." He dipped his finger in a glass of water, and as he just skimmed it over the lines, they vanished without a trace. The Student Anselmus felt as if some monster were throttling him: he could not utter a word. There stood he, with the unfortunate sheet in his hand; but Archivarius Lindhorst laughed aloud, and said: "Never mind, Herr Anselmus; what you could not do well before you will perhaps do better here. At any rate, you shall have better materials than you have been accustomed to. Begin, in Heaven's name!"

From a locked press, Archivarius Lindhorst now brought out a black fluid substance, which diffused a most peculiar odour; also pens, sharply pointed and of strange colour, together with a sheet of special whiteness and smoothness; then at last an Arabic manuscript: and as Anselmus sat down to work, the Archivarius left the room. The Student Anselmus had often copied Arabic manuscripts before; the first problem, therefore, seemed to him not so very difficult to solve.

"How those pot-hooks came into my fine English script, heaven and Archivarius Lindhorst know best," said he; "but that they are not from my hand, I will testify to the death!" At every new word that stood fair and perfect on the parchment, his courage increased, and with it his adroitness. In truth, these pens wrote exquisitely well; and the mysterious ink flowed pliantly, and black as jet, on the bright white parchment. And as he worked along so diligently, and with such strained attention, he began to feel more and more at home in the solitary room; and already he had quite fitted himself into his task, which he now hoped to finish well, when at the stroke of three the Archivarius called him into the side room to a savoury dinner. At table, Archivarius Lindhorst was in an especially good humour. He inquired about the Student Anselmus' friends, Conrector Paulmann and Registrator Heerbrand, and of the latter he had a store of merry anecdotes to tell. The good old Rhenish was particularly pleasing to the Student Anselmus, and made him more talkative than he usually was. At the stroke of four, he rose to resume his labour; and this punctuality appeared to please the Archivarius.

If the copying of these Arabic manuscripts had prospered in his hands before dinner, the task now went forward much better; indeed, he could not himself comprehend the rapidity and ease with which he succeeded in transcribing the twisted strokes of this foreign character. But it was as if, in his inmost soul, a voice were whispering in audible words: "Ah! could you accomplish it, if you were not thinking of her, if you did not believe in her and in her love?" Then there floated whispers, as in low, low, waving crystal tones, through the room: "I am near, near, near! I help you: be bold, be steadfast, dear Anselmus! I toil with you so that you may be mine!" And as, in the fullness of secret rapture, he caught these sounds, the unknown characters grew clearer and clearer to him; he scarcely needed to look at the original at all; nay, it was as if the letters were already standing in pale ink on the parchment, and he had nothing more to do but mark them black. So did he labour on, encompassed with dear inspiring tones as with soft sweet breath, till the clock struck six and Archivarius Lindhorst entered the apartment. He came forward to the table, with a singular smile; Anselmus rose in silence: the Archivarius still looked at him, with that mocking smile: but no sooner had he glanced over the copy, than the smile passed into deep solemn earnestness, which every feature of his face adapted itself to express. He seemed no longer the same. His eyes which usually gleamed with sparkling fire, now looked with unutterable mildness at Anselmus; a soft red tinted the pale cheeks; and instead of the irony which at other times compressed the mouth, the softly curved graceful lips now seemed to be opening for wise and soul-persuading speech. His whole form was higher, statelier; the wide nightgown spread itself like a royal mantle in broad folds over his breast and shoulders; and through the white locks, which lay on his high open brow, there wound a thin band of gold.

"Young man," began the Archivarius in solemn tone, "before you were aware of it, I knew you, and all the secret relations which bind you to the dearest and holiest of my interests!"

Serpentina loves you; a singular destiny, whose fateful threads were spun by enemies, is fulfilled, should she become yours and if you obtain, as an essential dowry, the Golden Flower Pot, which of right belongs to her. But only from effort and contest can your happiness in the higher life arise; hostile Principles assail you; and only the interior force with

65

which you withstand these contradictions can save you from disgrace and ruin. While labouring here, you are undergoing a season of instruction: belief and full knowledge will lead you to the near goal, if you but hold fast, what you have begun well. Bear her always and truly in your thoughts, her who loves you; then you will see the marvels of the Golden Pot, and be happy forevermore.

"Farewell! Archivarius Lindhorst expects you tomorrow at noon in his cabinet. Farewell!" With these words Archivarius Lindhorst softly pushed the Student Anselmus out of the door, which he then locked; and Anselmus found himself in the chamber where he had dined, the single door of which led out to the hallway.

Completely stupefied by these strange phenomena, the Student Anselmus stood lingering at the street door; he heard a window open above him, and looked up: it was Archivarius Lindhorst, quite the old man again, in his light-gray gown, as he usually appeared. The Archivarius called to him: "Hey, worthy Herr Anselmus, what are you studying over there? Tush, the Arabic is still in your head. My compliments to Herr Conrector Paulmann, if you see him; and come tomorrow precisely at noon. The fee for this day is lying in your right waistcoat pocket." The Student Anselmus actually found the speziesthaler in the pocket indicated; but he derived no pleasure from it. "What is to come of all this," said he to himself, "I do not know: but if it is some mad delusion and conjuring work that has laid hold of me, my dear Serpentina still lives and moves in my inward heart; and before I leave her, I will die; for I know that the thought in me is eternal, and no hostile Principle can take it from me: and what else is this thought but Serpentina's love?"

Seventh Vigil

At last Conrector Paulmann knocked the ashes out of his pipe, and said: "Now, then, it is time to go to bed." "Yes, indeed," replied Veronica, frightened at her father's sitting so late: for ten had struck long ago. No sooner, accordingly, had the Conrector withdrawn to his study and bedroom, and Franzchen's heavy breathing signified that she was asleep, than Veronica, who to save appearances had also gone to bed, rose softly, softly, out of it again, put on her clothes, threw her mantle round her, and glided out of doors.

Ever since the moment when Veronica had left old Liese, Anselmus had continually stood before her eyes; and it seemed as if a voice that was strange to her kept repeating in her soul that he was reluctant because he was held prisoner by an enemy and that Veronica, by secret means of the magic art, could break these bonds. Her confidence in old Liese grew stronger every day; and even the impression of unearthliness and horror by degrees became less, so that all the mystery and strangeness of her relation to the crone appeared before her only in the colour of something singular, romantic, and so not a little attractive. Accordingly, she had a firm purpose, even at the risk of being missed from home, and encountering a thousand inconveniences, to undertake the adventure of the Equinox. And now, at last, the fateful night, in which old Liese had promised to afford comfort and help, had come; and Veronica, long used to thoughts of nightly wandering, was full of heart and hope. She sped through the solitary streets; heedless of the storm which was howling in the air and dashing thick raindrops in her face.

With a stifled droning clang, the Kreuzthurm clock struck eleven, as Veronica, quite wet, reached old Liese's house. "Are you here, dear! wait, love; wait, love-" cried a voice from above; and in a moment the crone, laden with a basket, and attended by her cat, was also standing at the door. "We will go, then, and do what is proper, and can prosper in the night, which favours the work." So speaking, the crone with her cold hand seized the shivering Veronica, to whom she gave the heavy basket to carry, while she herself produced a little cauldron, a trivet, and a spade. By the time they reached the open fields, the rain had ceased, but the storm had become louder; howlings in a thousand tones were flitting through the air. A horrible heart-piercing lamentation sounded down from the black clouds, which rolled themselves together in rapid flight and veiled all things in thickest darkness. But the crone stepped briskly forward, crying in a shrill harsh voice: "Light, light, my lad!" Then blue forky gleams went quivering and sputtering before them; and Veronica perceived that it was the cat emitting sparks, and bounding forward to light the way; while his doleful ghastly screams were heard in the momentary pauses of the storm. Her heart almost failed; it was as if ice-cold talons were clutching into her soul; but, with a strong effort, she collected herself, pressed closer to the crone, and said: "It must all be accomplished now, come of it what may!"

"Right, right, little daughter!" replied the crone; "be

steady, like a good girl; you shall have something pretty, and Anselmus to boot."

At last the crone paused, and said: "Here is the place!" She dug a hole in the ground, then shook coals into it, put the trivet over them, and placed the cauldron on top of it. All this she accompanied with strange gestures, while the cat kept circling round her. From his tail there sputtered sparkles, which united into a ring of fire. The coals began to burn; and at last blue flames rose up around the cauldron. Veronica was ordered to lay off her mantle and veil, and to cower down beside the crone, who seized her hands, and pressed them hard, glaring with her fiery eyes at the maiden. Before long the strange materials (whether flowers, metals, herbs, or beasts, you could not determine), which the crone had taken from her basket and thrown into the cauldron, began to seethe and foam. The crone let go Veronica, then clutched an iron ladle, and plunged it into the glowing mass, which she began to stir, while Veronica, as she directed, was told to look steadfastly into the cauldron and fix her thoughts on Anselmus. Now the crone threw fresh ingredients, glittering pieces of metal, a lock of hair which Veronica had cut from her head, and a little ring which she had long worn, into the pot, while the old woman howled in dread, yelling tones through the gloom, and the cat, in quick, incessant motion, whimpered and whined--I wish very much, favorable reader, that on this twenty-third of September, you had been on the road to Dresden. In vain, when night sank down upon you, the people at the last stage-post tried to keep you there; the friendly host represented to you that the storm and the rain were too bitter, and moreover, for unearthly reasons, it was not safe to rush out into the dark on the night of the Equinox; but you paid no heed to him, thinking to yourself "I will give the postillion a whole thaler as a tip, and so, at latest, by one o'clock I shall reach Dresden. There in the Golden Angel or the Helmet or the City of Naumburg a good supper and a soft bed await me."

And now as you ride toward Dresden through the dark, you suddenly observe in the distance a very strange, flickering light. As you come nearer, you can distinguish a ring of fire, and in its center, beside a pot out of which a thick vapour is mounting with quivering red flashes and sparkles, there sit two very different forms. Right through the fire your road leads, but the horses snort, and stamp, and rear; the postillion curses and prays, and does not spare his whip; the horses will not stir from the spot. Without thinking, you leap out of the stagecoach and hasten forward toward the fire.

And now you clearly see a pretty girl, obviously of gentle birth, who is kneeling by the cauldron in a thin white nightdress. The storm has loosened her braids, and her long chestnut-brown hair is floating freely in the wind. Full in the dazzling light from the flame flickering from beneath the trivet hovers her sweet face; but in the horror which has poured over it like an icy stream, it is stiff and pale as death; and by her updrawn eyebrows, by her mouth, which is vainly opened for the shriek of anguish which cannot find its way from her bosom compressed with unnamable torment-you perceive her terror, her horror. She holds her small soft hands aloft, spasmodically pressed together, as if she were calling with prayers her guardian angel to deliver her from the monsters of the Pit, which, in obedience to this potent spell are to appear at any moment! There she kneels, motionless as a figure of marble. Opposite her a long, shrivelled, copper-yellow crone with a peaked hawk-nose and glistering cat-eyes sits cowering. From the black cloak which is huddled around her protrude her skinny naked arms; as she stirs the Hell-broth, she laughs and cries with creaking voice through the raging, bellowing storm.

I can well believe that unearthly feelings might have arisen in you, too--unacquainted though you are otherwise with fear and dread--at the aspect of this picture by Rembrandt or Hell-Breughel, taking place in actual life. Indeed, in horror, the hairs of your head might have stood on end. But your eye could not turn away from the gentle girl entangled in these infernal doings; and the electric stroke that quivered through all your nerves and fibres, kindled in you with the speed of lightning the courageous thought of defying the mysterious powers of the ring of fire; and at this thought your horror disappeared; nay, the thought itself came into being from your feelings of horror, as their product. Your heart felt as if you yourself were one of those guardian angels to whom the maiden, frightened almost to death, was praying; nay, as if you must instantly whip out your pocket pistol and without further ceremony blow the hag's brains out.

But while you were thinking of all of this most vividly,

you cried aloud, "Holla!" or "What the matter here?" or "What's going on there?" The postillion blew a clanging blast on his horn; the witch ladled about in her brewage, and in a trice everything vanished in thick smoke. Whether you would have found the girl, for whom you were groping in the darkness with the most heart-felt longing, I cannot say: but you surely would have destroyed the witch's spell and undone the magic circle into which Veronica had thoughtlessly entered..Alas! Neither you, favourable reader, nor any other man either drove or walked this way, on the twenty-third of September, in the tempestuous witch-favouring night; and Veronica had to abide by the cauldron, in deadly terror, till the work was near its close. She heard, indeed, the howling and raging around her; all sorts of hateful voices bellowed and bleated, and yelled and hummed; but she did not open her eyes, for she felt that the sight of the abominations and the horrors with which she was encircled might drive her into incurable destroying madness. The hag had ceased to stir the pot: its smoke grew fainter and fainter; and at last, nothing but a light spirit-flame was burning in the bottom. Then she cried:

"Veronica, my child! my darling! look into the grounds there! What do you see? What do you see?"

Veronica could not answer, yet it seemed as if all sorts of perplexing shapes were dancing and whirling in the cauldron; and suddenly, with friendly look, reaching her his hand, the Student Anselmus rose from the cavity of the vessel. She cried aloud: "It is Anselmus! It is Anselmus!"

Instantly the crone turned the cock fixed at the bottom of the cauldron, and glowing metal rushed forth, hissing and bubbling, into a little mould which she had placed beside it. The hag now sprang aloft, and shrieked, capering about with wild horrific gestures: "It is done! It is done!"

"Thanks, my pretty lad; did you watch?-Pooh, pooh, he is coming! Bite him to death! Bite him to death!" But then there sounded a strong rushing through the air: it was as if a huge eagle were pouncing down, striking round him with his pinions; and there shouted a tremendous voice:

"Hey, hey, vermin!-It is over! It is over!-Home with you!" The crone sank down with bitter howling, and Veronica's sense and recollection forsook her.

On her returning to herself, it was broad daylight, she was lying in her bed, and Fränzchen was standing before her with a cup of steaming tea and saying to her: "Tell me, sister, what in all the world ails you? I have been standing here this hour, and you have been lying senseless, as if in a fever, and moaning and whimpering so that we were frightened to death. Father has not gone to his class this morning because of you; he will be here directly with the doctor."

Veronica took the tea in silence: and while she was drinking it, the horrid images of the night rose vividly before her eyes. "So it was all nothing but a wild dream that tortured me? Yet last night, I surely went to that old woman; it was the twenty-third of September too? Well, I must have been very sick last night, and so fancied all this; and nothing has sickened me but my perpetual thinking of Anselmus and the strange old woman who gave herself out for Liese, but was no such thing, and only made a fool of me with that story."

Fränzchen, who had left the room, again came in with Veronica's mantle, all wet, in her hand.

"Look, sister," said she, "what a sight your mantle is! The storm last night blew open the shutters and upset the chair where your mantle was hanging; and the rain has come in, and wet it for you."

This speech sank heavy on Veronica's heart, for she now saw that it was no dream which had tormented her, but that she had really been with the witch. Anguish and horror took hold of her at the thought, and a fever-frost quivered through all her frame. In spasmodic shuddering, she drew the bedclothes close over her; but with this, she felt something hard pressing on her breast, and on grasping it with her hand, it seemed like a medallion: she drew it out, as soon as Fränzchen went away with the mantle; it was a little, round, bright-polished metallic mirror. "This is a present from the woman," cried she eagerly; and it was as if fiery beams were shooting from the mirror, and penetrating into her inmost soul with benignant warmth. The fever-frost was gone, and there streamed through her whole being an unutterable feeling of contentment and cheerful delight. She could not but remember Anselmus; and as she turned her thoughts more and more intensely on him, behold, he smiled on her in friendly fashion out of the mirror, like a living miniature portrait. But before long she felt as if it were no longer the image which she saw; no! but the Student Anselmus himself alive and in person. He was sitting in a stately chamber, with the strangest furniture, and diligently writing. Veronica was about to step forward, to pat his shoulder, and say to him: "Herr Anselmus, look round; it is I!" But she could not; for it was as if a fire-stream encircled him; and yet when she looked more narrowly, this fire-stream was nothing but large books with gilt leaves. At last Veronica so far succeeded that she caught Anselmus's eye: it seemed as if he needed, in gazing at her, to bethink himself who she was; but at last he smiled and said: "Ah! Is it you, dear Mademoiselle Paulmann! But why do you like now and then to take the form of a little snake?"

At these strange words, Veronica could not help laughing aloud; and with this she awoke as from a deep dream; and hastily concealed the little mirror, for the door opened, and Conrector Paulmann with Doctor Eckstein entered the room. Dr. Eckstein stepped forward to the bedside; felt Veronica's pulse with long profound study, and then said: "Ey! Ey!" Thereupon he wrote out a prescription; again felt the pulse; a second time said: "Ey! Ey!" and then left his patient. But from these disclosures of Dr. Eckstein's, Conrector Paulmann could not clearly make out what it was that ailed Veronica.

Eighth Vigil

The Student Anselmus had now worked several days with Archivarius Lindhorst; these working hours were for him the happiest of his life; still encircled with lovely tones, with Serpentina's encouraging voice, he was filled and overflowed with a pure delight, which often rose to highest rapture. Every difficulty, every little care of his needy existence, had vanished from his thoughts; and in the new life, which had risen on him as in serene sunny splendour, he comprehended all the wonders of a higher world, which before had filled him with astonishment, nay, with dread.

His copying proceeded rapidly and lightly; for he felt more and more as if he were writing characters long known to him; and he scarcely needed to cast his eye upon the manuscript, while copying it all with the greatest exactness.

Except at the hour of dinner, Archivarius Lindhorst seldom made his appearance; and this always precisely at the moment when Anselmus had finished the last letter of some manuscript: then the Archivarius would hand him another, and immediately leave him, without uttering a word; having first stirred the ink with a little black rod, and changed the old pens for new sharp-pointed ones. One day, when Anselmus, at the stroke of twelve, had as usual mounted the stair, he found the door through which he commonly entered, standing locked and Archivarius Lindhorst came forward from the other side, dressed in his strange flower-figured dressing gown.

He called aloud: "Today come this way, good Herr Anselmus; for we must go to the chamber where the masters of Bhagavadgita are waiting for us."

He stepped along the corridor, and led Anselmus through the same chambers and halls as at the first visit. The Student Anselmus again felt astonished at the marvellous beauty of the garden: but he now perceived that many of the strange flowers, hanging on the dark bushes, were in truth insects gleaming with lordly colours, hovering up and down with their little wings, as they danced and whirled in clusters, caressing one another with their antennae. On the other hand again, the rose and azure-coloured birds were odoriferous flowers; and the perfume which they scattered, mounted from their cups in low lovely tones, which, with the gurgling of distant fountains, and the sighing of the high groves and trees, mingled themselves into mysterious accords of a deep unutterable longing. The mock-birds, which had so jeered and flouted him before, were again fluttering to and fro over his head, and crying incessantly with their sharp small voices: "Herr Studiosus, Herr Studiosus, don't be in such a hurry! Don't peep into the clouds so! They may fall about your ears- He! He! Herr Studiosus, put your powdermantle on; cousin Screech-Owl will frizzle your toupee." And so it went along, in all manner of stupid chatter, till Anselmus left the garden.

Archivarius Lindhorst at last stepped into the azure chamber: the porphyry, with the Golden Flower Pot, was gone; instead of it, in the middle of the room, stood a table overhung with violet-coloured satin, upon which lay the writing gear already known to Anselmus; and a stuffed armchair, covered with the same sort of cloth, was placed beside it.

"Dear Herr Anselmus," said Archivarius Lindhorst, "you have now copied for me a number of manuscripts, rapidly and correctly, to my no small contentment: you have gained my confidence; but the hardest is still ahead; and that is the transcribing or rather painting of certain works, written in a peculiar character; I keep them in this room, and they can only be copied on the spot."

"You will, therefore, in future, work here; but I must recommend to you the greatest foresight and attention; a false stroke, or, which may Heaven forfend, a blot let fall on the original, will plunge you into misfortune."

Anselmus observed that from the golden trunks of the palm-tree, little emerald leaves projected: one of these leaves the Archivarius took hold of; and Anselmus saw that the leaf was in truth a roll of parchment, which the Archivarius unfolded, and spread out before the Student on the table. Anselmus wondered not a little at these strangely intertwisted characters; and as he looked over the many points, strokes, dashes, and twirls in the manuscript, he almost lost hope of ever copying it. He fell into deep thought on the subject.

"Be of courage, young man!" cried the Archivarius; "if you have continuing belief and true love, Serpentina will help you."

His voice sounded like ringing metal; and as Anselmus looked up in utter terror, Archivarius Lindhorst was standing before him in the kingly form, which, during the first visit, he had assumed in the library. Anselmus felt as if in his deep reverence he could not but sink on his knee; but the Archivarius stepped up the trunk of a palm-tree, and vanished aloft among the emerald leaves. The Student Anselmus perceived that the Prince of the Spirits had been speaking with him, and was now gone up to his study; perhaps intending, by the beams which some of the Planets had despatched to him as envoys, to send back word what was to become of Anselmus and Serpentina.

"It may be too," he further thought, "that he is expecting news from the springs of the Nile; or that some magician from Lapland is paying him a visit: it behooves me to set diligently about my task." And with this, he began studying the foreign characters on the roll of parchment.

The strange music of the garden sounded over him, and encircled him with sweet lovely odours; the mock-birds, too, he still heard giggling and twittering, but could not distinguish their words, a thing which greatly pleased him. At times also it was as if the leaves of the palm-trees were rustling, and as if the clear crystal tones, which Anselmus on that fateful Ascension Day had heard under the elder-bush, were beaming and flitting through the room. Wonderfully strengthened by this shining and tinkling, the Student Anselmus directed his eyes and thoughts more and more intensely on the superscription of the parchment roll; and before long he felt, as it were from his inmost soul, that the characters could denote nothing else than these words: Of

80

the marriage of the Salamander with the green snake. Then resounded a louder triphony of clear crystal bells: "Anselmus! dear Anselmus!" floated to him from the leaves; and, O wonder! on the trunk of the palm-tree the green snake came winding down.

"Serpentina! Serpentina!" cried Anselmus, in the madness of highest rapture; for as he gazed more earnestly, it was in truth a lovely glorious maiden that, looking at him with those dark blue eyes, lull of inexpressible longing, as they lived in his heart, was slowly gliding down to meet him. The leaves seemed to jut out and expand; on every hand were prickles sprouting from the trunk; but Serpentina twisted and wound herself deftly through them; and so drew her fluttering robe, glancing as if in changeful colours, along with her, that, plying round the dainty form, it nowhere caught on the projecting points and prickles of the palm-tree. She sat down by Anselmus on the same chair, clasping him with her arm, and pressing him towards her, so that he felt the breath which came from her lips, and the electric warmth of her frame.

"Dear Anselmus," began Serpentina, "you shall now be wholly mine; by your belief, by your love, you shall obtain me, and I will bring you the Golden Flower Pot, which shall make us both happy forevermore."

"O, kind, lovely Serpentina!" said Anselmus. "If I have you, what do I care for anything else! If you are but mine, I will joyfully give in to all the wonderful mysteries that have beset me since the moment when I first saw you."

81

"I know," continued Serpentina, "that the strange and mysterious things with which my father, often merely in the sport of his humour, has surrounded you have raised distrust and dread in your mind; but now, I hope, it shall be so no more; for I came at this moment to tell you, dear Anselmus, from the bottom of my heart and soul, everything, to the smallest detail, that you need to know fox understanding my father, and so for seeing clearly what your relation to him and to me really is."

Anselmus felt as if he were so wholly clasped and encircled by this gentle lovely form, that only with her could he move and live, and as if it were but the beating of her pulse that throbbed through his nerves and fibres; he listened to each one of her words till it sounded in his inmost heart, and, like a burning ray, kindled in him the rapture of Heaven. He had put his arm round that daintier than dainty waist; but the changeful glistering cloth of her robe was so smooth and slippery, that it seemed to him as if she could at any moment wind herself from his arms, and glide away. He trembled at the thought.

"Ah, do not leave me, gentlest Serpentina!" cried he; "you are my life."

"Not now," said Serpentina, "till I have told you everything that in your love of me you can comprehend:

"Know then, dearest, that my father is sprung from the wondrous race of the Salamanders; and that I owe my existence to his love for the green snake. In primeval times, in the Fairyland Atlantis, the potent Spirit-prince Phosphorus bore rule; and to him the Salamanders, and other spirits of the elements, were pledged by oath. Once upon a time, a Salamander, whom he loved before all others (it was my father), chanced to be walking in the stately garden, which Phosphorus' mother had decked in the lordliest fashion with her best gifts; and the Salamander heard a tall lily singing in low tones: 'Press down thy little eyelids, till my lover, the Morning-wind, awake thee.' He walked towards it: touched by his glowing breath, the lily opened her leaves: and he saw the lily's daughter, the green snake, lying asleep in the hollow of the flower."

Then was Salamander inflamed with warm love for the fair snake; and he carried her away from the lily, whose perfumes in nameless lamentation vainly called for her beloved daughter throughout all the garden. For the Salamander had borne her into the palace of Phosphorus and was there beseeching him: 'Wed me with my beloved, and she shall be mine forevermore.'-.'Madman, what do you ask?' said the Prince of the Spirits. 'Know that once the Lily was my mistress and bore rule with me; but the Spark, which I cast into her, threatened to annihilate the fair Lily; and only my victory over the black Dragon, whom now the Spirits of the Earth hold in fetters, maintains her, that her leaves continue strong enough to enclose this Spark and preserve it within them. But when you clasp the green snake, your fire will consume her frame; and a new being rapidly arising from her dust, will soar away and leave you.'

"The Salamander heeded not the warning of the Spirit-prince: full of longing ardour he folded the green snake in his arms; she crumbled into ashes; a winged being, born from her dust, soared away through the sky. Then the madness of desperation caught the Salamander; and he ran through the garden, dashing forth fire and flames; and wasted it in his wild fury, till its fairest flowers and blossoms hung down, blackened and scathed; and their lamentation filled the air."

The indignant Prince of the Spirits, in his wrath, laid hold of the Salamander, and said: 'Your fire has burnt out, your flames are extinguished, your rays darkened: sink down to the Spirits of the Earth; let them mock and jeer you, and keep you captive, till the Fire-elements shall again kindle, and beam up with you as with a new being from the Earth.' The poor Salamander sank down extinguished: but now the testy old earth-spirit, who was Phosphorus' gardener, came forth and said: 'Master! who has greater cause to complain of the Salamander than I? Had not all the fair flowers, which he has burnt, been decorated with my gayest metals; had I not stoutly nursed and tended them, and spent many a fair hue on their leaves? And yet I must pity the poor Salamander; for it was but love, in which you, O Master, have full often been entangled, that drove him to despair, and made him desolate the garden. Remit his too harsh punishment!'-'His fire is for the present extinguished,' said the Prince of the Spirits; 'but in the hapless time, when the speech of nature shall no longer be intelligible to degenerate man; when the spirits of the elements, banished into their own regions, shall speak to him only from afar, in faint, spent echoes; when, displaced from the harmonious circle, an infinite longing alone shall give him tidings of the land of marvels, which he once might inhabit while belief and love still dwelt in his soul: in this hapless time, the fire of the Salamander shall again kindle; but only to manhood shall he be permitted to rise, and entering wholly into many necessitous existence, he shall learn to endure its wants and oppressions. Yet not only shall the remembrance of his first state continue with him, but he shall again rise into the sacred harmony of all Nature; he shall understand its wonders, and the power of his fellow-spirits shall stand at his behest. Then, too, in a lily-bush, shall he find the green snake again: and the fruit of his marriage with her shall be three daughters, which, to men, shall appear in the form of their mother. In the spring season these shall disport themselves in the dark elder-bush, and sound with their lovely crystal voices.

And then if, in that needy and mean age of inward stuntedness, there shall be found a youth who understands their song; nay, if one of the little snakes look at him with her kind eyes; if the look awaken in him forecastings of the distant wondrous land, to which, having cast away the burden of the Common, he can courageously soar; if, with love to the snake, there rise in him belief in the wonders of nature, nay, in his own existence amid these wonders, then the snake shall be his.

But not till three youths of this sort have been found and wedded to the three daughters, may the Salamander cast away his heavy burden, and return to his brothers.'–'Permit me,

Master,' said the earth-spirit, to make these three daughters a present, which may glorify their life with the husbands they shall find. Let each of them receive from me a flower pot, of the fairest metal which I have; I will polish it with beams borrowed from the diamond; in its glitter shall our kingdom of wonders, as it now exists in the harmony of universal nature be imaged back in glorious dazzling reflection; and from its interior, on the day of marriage, shall spring forth a fire-lily, whose eternal blossoms shall encircle the youth that is found worthy, with sweet wafting odours. Soon too shall he learn its speech, and understand the wonders of our kingdom, and dwell with his beloved in Atlantis itself.'

"Thou perceivest well, dear Anselmus, that the Salamander of whom I speak is no other than my father. In spite of his higher nature, he was forced to subject himself to the paltriest contradictions of common life; and hence, indeed, often comes the wayward humour with which he vexes many. He has told me now and then, that, for the inward make of mind, which the Spirit-prince Phosphorus required as a condition of marriage with me and my sisters, men have a name at present, which, in truth, they frequently enough misapply: they call it a childlike poetic character. This character, he says, is often found in youths, who, by reason of their high sim-plicity of manners, and their total want of what is called knowledge of the world, are mocked by the common mob. Ah, dear Anselmus! beneath the elder-bush, you understood my song, my look: you love the green snake, you believe in me, and will be mine for evermore! The fair lily will bloom forth from the Golden Flower Pot; and we shall dwell, happy, and united, and blessed, in Atlantis together!

"Yet I must not hide from you that in its deadly battle with the Salamanders and spirits of the earth, the black Dragon burst from their grasp, and hurried off through the air. Phosphorus, indeed, again holds him in fetters; but from the black quills, which, in the struggle, rained down on the ground, there sprang up hostile spirits, which on all hands set themselves against the Salamanders and spirits of the earth. That woman who hates you so, dear Anselmus, and who, as my father knows full well, is striving for possession of the Golden Flower Pot; that woman owes her existence to the love of such a quill (plucked in battle from the Dragon's wing) for a certain beet beside which it dropped. She knows her origin and her power; for, in the moans and convulsions of the captive Dragon, the secrets of many a mysterious constellation are revealed to her; and she uses every means and effort to work from the outward into the inward and unseen; while my father, with the beams which shoot forth from the spirit of the Salamander, withstands and subdues her. All the baneful principles which lurk in deadly herbs and poisonous beasts, she collects; and, mixing them under favourable constellations, raises therewith many a wicked spell, which overwhelms the soul of man with fear and trembling, and subjects him to the power of those demons, produced from the Dragon when it yielded in battle. Beware of that old woman, dear Anselmus! She hates you, because your childlike pious character has annihilated many of her wicked charms. Keep true, true to me; soon you will be at the goal!"

"O my Serpentina! my own Serpentina!" cried the Student Anselmus, "how could I leave you, how should I not love you forever!" A kiss was burning on his lips; he awoke as from a deep dream: Serpentina had vanished; six o'clock was striking, and it fell heavy on his heart that today he had not copied a single stroke. Full of anxiety, and dreading reproaches from the Archivarius, he looked into the sheet; and, O wonder! the copy of the mysterious manuscript was fairly concluded; and he thought, on viewing the characters more narrowly, that the writing was nothing else but Serpentina's story of her father, the favourite of the Spirit-prince Phosphorus, in Atlantis, the land of marvels. And now entered Archivarius Lindhorst, in his light-gray surtout, with hat and staff: he looked into the parchment on which Anselmus had been writing; took a large pinch of snuff, and said with a smile: "Just as I thought!-Well, Herr Anselmus, here is your speziesthaler; we will now go to the Linkische Bath: please follow me!" The Archivarius walked rapidly through the garden, in which there was such a din of singing, whistling, talking, that the Student Anselmus was quite deafened with it, and thanked Heaven when he found himself on the street..Scarcely had they walked twenty paces, when they met Registrator Heerbrand, who companionably joined them. At the Gate, they filled their pipes, which they had upon them:

Registrator Heerbrand complained that he had left his

tinder-box behind, and could not strike fire. "Fire!" cried Archivarius Lindhorst, scornfully; "here is fire enough, and to spare!" And with this he snapped his fingers, out of which came streams of sparks, and directly kindled the pipes.-"Observe the chemical knack of some men!" said Registrator Heerbrand; but the Student Anselmus thought, not without internal awe, of the Salamander and his history.

In the Linkische Bath, Registrator Heerbrand drank so much strong double beer, that at last, though usually a good-natured quiet man, he began singing student songs in squeaking tenor; he asked everyone sharply, whether he was his friend or not? and at last had to be taken home by the Student Anselmus, long after the Archivarius Lindhorst had gone his ways.

Ninth Vigil

The strange and mysterious things which day by day befell the Student Anselmus, had entirely withdrawn him from his customary life. He no longer visited any of his friends, and waited every morning with impatience for the hour of noon, which was to unlock his paradise. And yet while his whole soul was turned to the gentle Serpentina, and the wonders of Archivarius Lindhorst's fairy kingdom, he could not help now and then thinking of Veronica; nay, often it seemed as if she came before him and confessed with blushes how heartily she loved him; how much she longed to rescue him from the phantoms, which were mocking and befooling him. At times he felt as if a foreign power, suddenly breaking in on his mind, were drawing him with resistless force to the forgotten Veronica; as if he must needs follow her whither she pleased to lead him, nay, as if he were bound to her by ties that would not break. That very night after Serpentina had first appeared to him in the form of a lovely maiden; after the wondrous secret of the Salamander's nuptials with the green snake had been disclosed, Veronica came before him more vividly than ever. Nay, not till he awoke, was he clearly aware that he had only been dreaming; for he had felt persuaded that Veronica was actually beside him, complaining with an expression of keen sorrow, which pierced through his inmost soul, that he should sacrifice her deep true love to fantastic visions, which only the distemper of his mind called into being, and which, moreover, would at last prove his ruin.

Veronica was lovelier than he had ever seen her; he could not drive her from his thoughts: and in this perplexed and contradictory mood he hastened out, hoping to get rid of it by a morning walk.

A secret magic influence led him on the Pirna gate: he was just turning into a cross street, when Conrector Paulmann, coming after him, cried out: "Ey! Ey!-Dear Herr Anselmus!--Amice! Amice! Where, in Heaven's name, have you been buried so long? We never see you at all. Do you know, Veronica is longing very much to have another song with you. So come along; you were just on the road to me, at any rate."

The Student Anselmus, constrained by this friendly violence, went along with the Conrector.

On entering the house, they were met by Veronica, attired with such neatness and attention, that Conrector Paulmann, full of amazement, asked her: "Why so decked, Mamsell? Were you expecting visitors? Well, here I bring you Herr Anselmus."

The Student Anselmus, in daintily and elegantly kissing Veronica's hand, felt a small soft pressure from it, which shot like a stream of fire over all his frame. Veronica was cheerfulness, was grace itself; and when Paulmann left them for his study, she contrived, by all manner of rogueries and waggeries, to uplift the Student Anselmus so much that he at last quite forgot his bashfulness, and jigged round the room with the playful girl. But here again the demon of awkwardness got hold of him: he jolted on a table, and

Veronica's pretty little workbox fell to the floor. Anselmus lifted it; the lid had flown up; and a little round metallic mirror was glittering on him, into which he looked with peculiar delight. Veronica glided softly up to him; laid her hand on his arm, and pressing close to him, looked over his shoulder into the mirror also. And now Anselmus felt as if a battle were beginning in his soul: thoughts, images flashed out--Archivarius Lindhorst-Serpentina-the green snake-at last the tumult abated, and all this chaos arranged and shaped itself into distinct consciousness. It was now clear to him that he had always thought of Veronica alone; nay, that the form which had yesterday appeared to him in the blue chamber, had been no other than Veronica; and that the wild legend of the Salamander's marriage with the green snake had merely been written down by him from the manuscript, but nowise related in his hearing. He wondered greatly at all these dreams; and ascribed them solely to the heated state of mind into which Veronica's love had brought him, as well as to his working with Archivarius Lindhorst, in whose rooms there were, besides, so many strangely intoxicating odours. He could not help laughing heartily at the mad whim of falling in love with a little green snake; and taking a well-fed Privy Archivarius for a Salamander: "Yes, yes! It is Veronica!" cried he aloud; but on turning round his head, he looked right into Veronica's blue eyes, from which warmest love was beaming. A faint soft Ah! escaped her lips, which at that moment were burning on his.

"O happy I!" sighed the enraptured Student: "What I

yesternight but dreamed, is in very deed mine today."

"But will you really marry me, then, when you are a Hofrath?" said Veronica.

"That I will," replied the Student Anselmus; and just then the door creaked, and Conrector Paulmann entered with the words:

"Now, dear Herr Anselmus, I will not let you go today. You will put up with a bad dinner; then Veronica will make us delightful coffee, which we shall drink with Registrator Heerbrand, for he promised to come here."

"Ah, Herr Conrector!" answered the Student Anselmus, "are you not aware that I must go to Archivarius Lindhorst's and copy?"

"Look, Amice!" said Conrector Paulmann, holding up his watch, which pointed to half-past twelve.

The Student Anselmus saw clearly that he was much too late for Archivarius Lindhorst; and he complied with the Conrector's wishes the more readily, as he might now hope to look at Veronica the whole day long, to obtain many a stolen glance, and little squeeze of the hand, nay, even to succeed in conquering a kiss. So high had the Student Anselmus's desires now mounted; he felt more and more contented in soul, the more fully he convinced himself that he should soon be delivered from all these fantasies, which really might have made a sheer idiot of him.

Registrator Heerbrand came, as he had promised, after dinner; and coffee being over, and the dusk come on, the Registrator, puckering his face together, and gaily rubbing his hands, signified that he had something about him, which, if mingled and reduced to form, as it were, paged and titled, by Veronica's fair hands, might be pleasant to them all, on this October evening.

"Come out, then, with this mysterious substance which you carry with you, most valued Registrator," cried Conrector Paulmann. Then Registrator Heerbrand shoved his hand into his deep pocket, and at three journeys, brought out a bottle of arrack, two lemons, and a quantity of sugar. Before half an hour had passed, a savoury bowl of punch was smoking on Paulmann's table. Veronica drank their health in a sip of the liquor; and before long there was plenty of gay, good-natured chat among the friends. But the Student Anselmus, as the spirit of the drink mounted into his head, felt all the images of those wondrous things, which for some time he had experienced, again coming through his mind. He saw the Archivarius in his damask dressing gown, which glittered like phosphorus; he saw the azure room, the golden palm-trees; nay, it now seemed to him as if he must still believe in Serpentina: there was a fermentation, a conflicting tumult in his soul. Veronica handed him a glass of punch; and in taking it, he gently touched her hand. "Serpentina! Veronica!" sighed he to himself. He sank into deep dreams; but Registrator Heerbrand cried quite aloud: "A strange old gentleman, whom nobody can fathom, he is and will be, this Archivarius Lindhorst. Well, long life to him! Your glass, Herr Anselmus!"

Then the Student Anselmus awoke from his dreams, and

said, as he touched glasses with Registrator Heerbrand: "That proceeds, respected Herr Registrator, from the circumstance, that Archivarius Lindhorst is in reality a Salamander, who in his fury laid waste the Spirit-prince Phosphorus' garden, because the green snake had flown away from him."

"What?" inquired Conrector Paulmann.

"Yes," continued the Student Anselmus; "and for this reason he is now forced to be a Royal Archivarius; and to keep house here in Dresden with his three daughters, who, after all, are nothing more than little gold-green snakes, that bask in elder-bushes, and traitorously sing, and seduce away young people, like so many sirens."

"Herr Anselmus! Herr Anselmus!" cried Conrector Paulmann, "is there a crack in your brain? In Heaven's name, what monstrous stuff is this you are babbling?"

"He is right," interrupted Registrator Heerbrand: "that fellow, that Archivarius, is a cursed Salamander, and strikes you fiery snips from his fingers, which burn holes in your surtout like red-hot tinder. Ay, ay, you are in the right, brotherkin Anselmus; and whoever says No, is saying No to me!" And at these words Registrator Heerbrand struck the table with his fist, till the glasses rung again.

"Registrator! Are you raving mad?" cried the enraged Conrector. "Herr Studiosus, Herr Studiosus! what is this you are about again?"

"Ah!" said the Student, "you too are nothing but a bird, a screech-owl, that frizzles toupees, Herr Conrector!"

"What?-I a bird?-A screech-owl, a frizzier?" cried the

Conrector, full of indignation: "Sir, you are mad, born mad!"

"But the crone will get a clutch of him," cried Registrator Heerbrand.

"Yes, the crone is potent," interrupted the Student Anselmus, "though she is but of mean descent; for her father was nothing but a ragged wing-feather, and her mother a dirty beet: but the most of her power she owes to all sorts of baneful creatures, poisonous vermin which she keeps about her."

"That is a horrid calumny," cried Veronica, with eyes all glowing in anger: "old Liese is a wise woman; and the black cat is no baneful creature, but a polished young gentleman of elegant manners, and her cousin-german."

"Can he eat Salamanders without singeing his whiskers, and dying like a snuffed candle?" cried Registrator Heerbrand.

"No! no!" shouted the Student Anselmus, "that he never can in this world; and the green snake loves me, and I have looked into Serpentina's eyes."

"The cat will scratch them out," cried Veronica..."Salamander, Salamander beats them all, all," hallooed Conrector Paulmann, in the highest fury: "But am I in a madhouse? Am I mad myself? What foolish nonsense am I chattering? Yes, I am mad too! mad too!" And with this, Conrector Paulmann started up; tore the peruke from his head, and dashed it against the ceiling of the room; till the battered locks whizzed, and, tangled into utter disorder, it rained down powder far and wide. Then the Student Anselmus and Registrator Heerbrand seized the punch-bowl and the glasses; and, hallooing and huzzaing, pitched them against the ceiling also, and the sherds fell jingling and tingling about their ears.

"Vivat the Salamander!-Pereat, pereat the crone!-Break the metal mirror!-Dig the cat's eyes out!-Bird, little bird, from the air-Eheu-Eheu-Evoe-Evoe, Salamander!" So shrieked, and shouted, and bellowed the three, like utter maniacs. With loud weeping, Franzchen ran out; but Veronica lay whimpering for pain and sorrow on the sofa.

At this moment the door opened: all was instantly still; and a little man, in a small gray cloak, came stepping in. His countenance had a singular air of gravity; and especially the round hooked nose, on which was a huge pair of spectacles, distinguished itself from all noses ever seen. He wore a strange peruke too; more like a feather-cap than a wig.

"Ey, many good-evenings!" grated and cackled the little comical mannikin. "Is the Student Herr Anselmus among you, gentlemen?-Best compliments from Archivarius Lindhorst; he has waited today in vain for Herr Anselmus; but tomorrow he begs most respectfully to request that Herr Anselmus does not miss the hour."

And with this, he went out again; and all of them now saw clearly that the grave little mannikin was in fact a gray parrot. Conrector Paulmann and Registrator Heerbrand raised a horselaugh, which reverberated through the room; and in the intervals, Veronica was moaning and whimpering, as if torn by nameless sorrow; but, as to the Student Anselmus, the madness of inward horror was darting through him; and unconsciously he ran through the door, along the streets. Instinctively he reached his house, his garret. Ere long Veronica came in to him, with a peaceful and friendly look, and asked him why, in the festivity, he had so vexed her; and desired him to be upon his guard against figments of the imagination while working at Archivarius Lindhorst's. "Goodnight, goodnight, my beloved friend!" whispered Veronica scarcely audibly, and breathed a kiss on his lips. He stretched out his arms to clasp her, but the dreamy shape had vanished, and he awoke cheerful and refreshed. He could not but laugh heartily at the effects of the punch; but in thinking of Veronica, he felt pervaded by a most delightful feeling. "To her alone," said he within himself, "do I owe this return from my insane whims. Indeed, I was little better than the man who believed himself to be of glass; or the one who did not dare leave his room for fear the hens should eat him, since he was a barleycorn. But so soon as I am Hofrath, I shall marry Mademoiselle Paulmann, and be happy, and there's an end to it."

At noon, as he walked through Archivarius Lindhorst's garden, he could not help wondering how all this had once appeared so strange and marvellous. He now saw nothing that was not common; earthen flowerpots, quantities of geraniums, myrtles, and the like. Instead of the glittering multi-coloured birds which used to flout him, there were nothing but a few sparrows, fluttering hither and thither, which raised an unpleasant unintelligible cry at sight of Anselmus.

The azure room also had quite a different look; and he could not understand how that glaring blue, and those unnatural golden trunks of palm-trees, with their shapeless glistening leaves, should ever have pleased him for a moment. The Archivarius looked at him with a most peculiar ironic smile, and asked: "Well, how did you like the punch last night, good Anselmus?" "Ah, doubtless you have heard from the gray parrot how—" answered the Student Anselmus, quite ashamed; but he stopped short, thinking that this appearance of the parrot was all a piece of jugglery.

"I was there myself," said Archivarius Lindhorst; "didn't you see me? But, among the mad pranks you were playing, I almost got lamed: for I was sitting in the punch bowl, at the very moment when Registrator Heerbrand laid hands on it, to dash it against the ceiling; and I had to make a quick retreat into the Conrector's pipehead. Now, adieu, Herr Anselmus! Be diligent at your task; for the lost day you shall also have a speziesthaler, because you worked so well before."

"How can the Archivarius babble such mad stuff?" thought the Student Anselmus, sitting down at the table to begin the copying of the manuscript, which Archivarius Lindhorst had as usual spread out before him. But on the parchment roll, he perceived so many strange crabbed strokes and twirls all twisted together in inexplicable confusion, offering no resting point for the eye, that it seemed to him well nigh impossible to copy all this exactly. Nay, in glancing over the whole, you might have thought the parchment was nothing but a piece of thickly veined marble, or a stone sprinkled over with lichens. Nevertheless he determined to do his utmost; and boldly dipped in his pen: but the ink would not run, do what he liked; impatiently he flicked the point of his pen against his fingernail, and-Heaven and Earth!-a huge blot fell on the outspread orig-inal!

Hissing and foaming, a blue flash rose from the blot; and crackling and wavering, shot through the room to the ceiling. Then a thick vapour rolled from the walls; the leaves began to rustle, as if shaken by a tempest; and down out of them darted glaring basilisks in sparkling fire; these kindled the vapour, and the bickering masses of flame rolled round Anselmus. The golden trunks of the palm-trees became gigantic snakes, which knocked their frightful heads together with piercing metallic clang; and wound their scaly bodies round Anselmus.

"Madman! suffer now the punishment of what, in capricious irreverence, thou hast done!" cried the frightful voice of the crowned Salamander, who appeared above the snakes like a glittering beam in the midst of the flame: and now the yawning jaws of the snakes poured forth cataracts of fire on Anselmus; and it was as if the fire-streams were congealing about his body, and changing into a firm ice-cold mass. But while Anselmus's limbs, more and more pressed together, and contracted, stiffened into powerlessness, his senses passed away. On returning to himselg he could not stir a joint: he was as if surrounded with a glistening brightness, on which he struck if he but tried to lift his hand.-Alas! He was sitting in a well-corked crystal bottle, on a shelf in the library of Archivarius Lindhorst.

Tenth Vigil

I am probably right in doubting, gracious reader, that you were ever sealed up in a glass bottle, or even that you have ever been oppressed with such sorcery in your most vivid dreams. If you have had such dreams, you will understand the Student Anselmus's woe and will feel it keenly enough; but if you have not, then your flying imagination, for the sake of Anselmus and me, will have to be obliging enough to enclose itself for a few moments in the crystal. You are drowned in dazzling splendour; everything around you appears illuminated and begirt with beaming rainbow hues: in the sheen everything seems to quiver and waver and clang and drone. You are swimming, but you are powerless and cannot move, as if you were imbedded in a firmly congealed ether which squeezes you so tightly that it is in vain that your spirit commands your dead and stiffened body. Heavier and heavier the mountainous burden lies on you; more and more every breath exhausts the tiny bit of air that still plays up and down in the tight space around you; your pulse throbs madly; and cut through with horrid anguish, every nerve is quivering and bleeding in your dead agony.

Favourable reader, have pity on the Student Anselmus! This inexpressible torture seized him in his glass prison: but he felt too well that even death could not release him, for when he had fainted with pain, he awoke again to new wretchedness when the morning sun shone into the room. He could move no limb, and his thoughts struck against the glass, stunning him with discordant clang; and instead of the words which the spirit used to speak from within him he now heard only the stifled din of madness. Then he exclaimed in his despair: "O Serpentina! Serpentina! Save me from this agony of Hell!" And it was as if faint sighs breathed around him, which spread like transparent green elder-leaves over the glass; the clanging ceased; the dazzling, perplexing glitter was gone, and he breathed more freely.

"Haven't I myself solely to blame for my misery? Ah! Haven't I sinned against you, kind, beloved Serpentina? Haven't I raised vile doubts of you? Haven't I lost my belief, and with it, all, all that was to make me so blessed? Ah! You will now never, never be mine; for me the Golden Pot is lost, and I shall not behold its wonders any more. Ah, could I but see you but once more; but once more hear your kind, sweet voice, lovely Serpentina!"

So wailed the Student Anselmus, caught with deep piercing sorrow: then a voice spoke close by him: "What the devil ails you, Herr Studiosus? What makes you lament so, out of all compass and measure?"

The Student Anselmus now perceived that on the same shelf with him were five other bottles, in which he perceived three Kreuzkirche Scholars, and two Law Clerks.

"Ah, gentlemen, my fellows in misery," cried he, "how is it possible for you to be so calm, nay, so happy, as I read in your cheerful looks? You are sitting here corked up in glass bottles, as well as I, and cannot move a finger, nay, not think a reasonable thought, but there rises such a murder-tumult of clanging and droning, and in your head itself a tumbling and rumbling enough to drive one mad. But of course you do not believe in the Salamander, or the green snake."

"You are pleased to jest, Mein Herr Studiosus," replied a Kreuzkirche Scholar; "we have never been better off than at present: for the speziesthalers which the mad Archivarius gave us for all kinds of pot-book copies, are chinking in our pockets; we have now no Italian choruses to learn by heart; we go every day to Joseph's or other beer gardens, where the double-beer is sufficient, and we can look a pretty girl in the face; so we sing like real Students, Gaudeamus igitur, and are contented!"

"They of the Cross are quite right," added a Law Clerk; "I too am well furnished with speziesthalers, like my dearest colleague beside me here; and we now diligently walk about on the Weinberg, instead of scurvy law-copying within four walls."

"But, my best, worthiest masters!" said the Student Anselmus, "do you not observe, then, that you are all and sundry corked up in glass bottles, and cannot for your hearts walk a hairsbreadth?"

Here the Kreuzkirche Scholars and the Law Clerks set up a loud laugh, and cried: "The Student is mad; he fancies himself to be sitting in a glass bottle, and is standing on the Elbe Bridge and looking right down into the water. Let us go on our way!"

"Ah!" sighed the Student, "they have never seen the kind Serpentina; they do not know what Freedom, and life in Love, and Belief, signify; and so by reason of their folly and low-mindedness, they do not feel the oppression of the imprisonment into which the Salamander has cast them. But I, unhappy I, must perish in want and woe, if she whom I so inexpressibly love does not rescue me!"

Then, waving in faint tinkles, Serpentina's voice flitted through the room: "Anselmus! Believe, love, hope!" And every tone beamed into Anselmus's prison; and the crystal yielded to his pressure and expanded, till the breast of the captive could move and heave.

The torment of his situation became less and less, and he saw clearly that Serpentina still loved him; and that it was she alone, who had rendered his confinement tolerable. He disturbed himself no more about his inane companions in misfortune; but directed all his thoughts and meditations on the gentle Serpentina. Suddenly, however, there arose on the other side a dull, croaking repulsive murmur. Before long he could observe that it came from an old coffeepot, with half-broken lid, standing opposite him on a little shelf. As he looked at it more narrowly, the ugly features of a wrinkled old woman unfolded themselves gradually; and in a few moments the Apple-wife of the Schwarzthor stood before him. She grinned and laughed at him, and cried with screeching voice:

"Ey, ey, my pretty boy, must you lie in limbo now? In the crystal you ended! Didn't I tell you so long ago?"

"Mock and jeer me, you cursed witch!" said Anselmus, "you are to blame for it all; but the Salamander will catch you, you vile beet!"

"Ho, ho!" replied the crone, "not so proud, my fine copyist. You have squashed my little sons and you have scarred my nose; but I still love you, you knave, for once you were a pretty fellow, and my little daughter likes you, too. Out of the crystal you will never get unless I help you: I cannot climb up there, but my friend the rat, that lives close behind you, will eat the shelf in two; you will jingle down, and I shall catch you in my apron so that your nose doesn't get broken or your fine sleek face get injured at all. Then I will carry you to Mamsell Veronica, and you shall marry her when you become Hofrath."

"Get away, you devil's brood!" shouted the Student Anselmus in fury. "It was you alone and your hellish arts that made me commit the sin which I must now expiate. But I will bear it all patiently: for only here can I be encircled with Serpentina's love and consolation. Listen to me, you hag, and despair! I defy your power: I love Serpentina and none but her forever. I will not become Hofrath, I will not look at Veronica; by your means she is enticing me to evil. If the green snake cannot be mine, I will die in sorrow and longing. Away, filthy buzzard!"

The crone laughed, till the chamber rang: "Sit and die then," cried she: "but now it is time to set to work; for I have other trade to follow here." She threw off her black cloak, and so stood in hideous nakedness; then she ran round in circles, and large folios came tumbling down to her; out of these she tore parchment leaves, and rapidly patching them

105

together in artful combination, and fixing them on her body, in a few instants she was dressed as if in strange multi-colored armor. Spitting fire, the black cat darted out of the ink-glass, which was standing on the table, and ran mewing towards the crone, who shrieked in loud triumph, and along with him vanished through the door.

Anselmus observed that she went towards the azure chamber; and directly he heard a hissing and storming in the distance; the birds in the garden were crying; the Parrot creaked out: "Help! help! Thieves! thieves!" That moment the crone returned with a bound into the room, carrying the Golden Flower Pot on her arm, and with hideous gestures, shrieking wildly through the air; "Joy! joy, little son!-Kill the green snake! To her, son! To her!"

Anselmus thought he heard a deep moaning, heard Serpentina's voice. Then horror and despair took hold of him: he gathered all his force, he dashed violently, as if every nerve and artery were bursting, against the crystal; a piercing clang went through the room, and the Archivarius in his bright damask dressing gown was standing in the door.

"Hey, hey! vermin!-Mad spell!-Witchwor!-Here, holla!" So shouted he: then the black hair of the crone started up in tufts; her red eyes glanced with infernal fire, and clenching together the peaked fangs of her abominable jaws, she hissed: "Hiss, at him! Hiss, at him! Hiss!" and laughed and neighed in scorn and mockery, and pressed the Golden Flower Pot firmly to her, and threw out of it handfuls of glittering earth on the Archivarius; but as it touched the dressing gown, the earth changed into flowers, which rained down on the ground. Then the lilies of the dressing gown flickered and flamed up; and the Archivarius caught these lilies blazing in sparky fire and dashed them on the witch; she howled with agony, but as she leaped aloft and shook her armor of parchment the lilies went out, and fell away into ashes.

"To her, my lad!" creaked the crone: then the black cat darted through the air, and bounded over the Archivarius's head towards the door; but the gray parrot fluttered out against him; caught him by the nape with his crooked bill, till red fiery blood burst down over his neck; and Serpentina's voice cried: "Saved! Saved!" Then the crone, foaming with rage and desperation, darted at the Archivarius: she threw the Golden Flower Pot behind her, and holding up the long talons of her skinny fists, tried to clutch the Archivarius by the throat: but he instantly doffed his dressing gown, and hurled it against her. Then, hissing, and sputtering, and bursting, blue flames shot from the parchment leaves, and the crone rolled around howling in agony, and strove to get fresh earth from the Flower Pot, fresh parchment leaves from the books, that she might stifle the blazing flames; and whenever any earth or leaves came down on her, the flames went out. But now, from the interior of the Archivarius issued fiery crackling beams, which darted on the crone.

"Hey, hey! To it again! Salamander! Victory!" clanged the Archivarius's voice through the chamber; and a hundred bolts whirled forth in fiery circles round the shrieking crone. Whizzing and buzzing flew cat and parrot in their furious battle; but at last the parrot, with his strong wing, dashed the cat to the ground; and with his talons transfixing and holding fast his adversary, which, in deadly agony, uttered horrid mews and howls, he, with his sharp bill, picked out his glowing eyes, and the burning froth spouted from them. Then thick vapour streamed up from the spot where the crone, hurled to the ground, was lying under the dressing gown: her howling, her terrific, piercing cry of lamentation, died away in the remote distance. The smoke, which had spread abroad with penetrating stench, cleared away; the Archivarius picked up his dressing gown; and under it lay an ugly beet.

"Honoured Herr Archivarius, here let me offer you the vanquished foe," said the parrot, holding out a black hair in his beak to Archivarius Lindhorst.

"Very right, my worthy friend," replied the Archivarius: "here lies my vanquished foe too: be so good now as manage what remains. This very day, as a small douceur, you shall have six coconuts, and a new pair of spectacles also, for I see the cat has villainously broken the glasses of these old ones."

"Yours forever, most honoured friend and patron!" answered the parrot, much delighted; then took the withered beet in his bill, and fluttered out with it by the window, which Archivarius Lindhorst had opened for him.

The Archivarius now lifted the Golden Flower Pot, and cried, with a strong voice, "Serpentina! Serpentina!" But as the Student Anselmus, rejoicing in the destruction of the vile witch who had hurried him into misfortune, cast his eyes on the Archivarius, behold, here stood once more the high majestic form of the Spirit-prince, looking up to him with indescribable dignity and grace..."Anselmus," said the Spirit-prince, "not you, but a hostile principle, which strove destructively to penetrate into your nature, and divide you against yourself, was to blame for your unbelief."

"You have kept your faithfulness: be free and happy." A bright flash quivered through the spirit of Anselmus: the royal triphony of the crystal bells sounded stronger and louder than he had ever heard it: his nerves and fibres thrilled; but, swelling higher and higher, the melodious tones rang through the room; the glass which enclosed Anselmus broke; and he rushed into the arms of his dear and gentle Serpentina.

Eleventh Vigil

"**But** tell me, best Registrator! how could the cursed punch last night mount into our heads, and drive us to all kinds of allotria?" So said Conrector Paulmann, as he next morning entered his room, which still lay full of broken sherds; with his hapless peruke, dissolved into its original elements, soaked in punch among the ruin. For after the Student Anselmus ran out, Conrector Paulmann and Registrator Heerbrand had kept trotting and hobbling up and down the room, shouting like maniacs, and butting their heads together; till Franzchen, with much labour, carried her dizzy papa to bed; and Registrator Heerbrand, in the deepest exhaustion, sank on the sofa, which Veronica had left, taking refuge in her bedroom. Registrator Heerbrand had his blue handkerchief tied about his head; he looked quite pale and melancholic, and moaned out: "Ah, worthy Conrector, it was not the punch which Mamsell Veronica most admirably brewed, no! but it was simply that cursed Student who was to blame for all the mischief. Do you not observe that he has long been mente captus? And are you not aware that madness is infectious? One fool makes twenty; pardon me, it is an old proverb: especially when you have drunk a glass or two, you fall into madness quite readily, and then involuntarily you manoeuvre, and go through your exercise, just as the crack-brained fugleman makes the motion. Would you believe it Conrector? I am still giddy when I think of that gray parrot!"

"Gray fiddlestick!" interrupted the Conrector: "it was

nothing but Archivarius Lindhorst's little old Famulus, who had thrown a gray cloak over himself, and was looking for the Student Anselmus."

"It may be," answered Registrator Heerbrand; "but, I must confess, I am quite downcast in spirit; the whole night through there was such a piping and organing."

"That was I," said the Conrector, "for I snore loud."

"Well, may be," answered the Registrator: "but, Conrector, Conrector! I had reason to raise some cheerfulness among us last night-And that Anselmus spoiled it all! You do not know-O Conrector, Conrector!" And with this, Registrator Heerbrand started up; plucked the cloth from his head, embraced the Conrector, warmly pressed his hand, and again cried, in quite heart-breaking tone: "O Conrector, Conrector!" and snatching his hat and staff, rushed out of doors.

"This Anselmus will not cross my threshold again," said Conrector Paulmann; "for I see very well, that, with this moping madness of his, he robs the best gentlemen of their senses. The Registrator has now gone overboard, too: I have hitherto kept safe; but the Devil, who knocked hard last night in our carousal, may get in at last, and play his tricks with me. So Apage, Satanas! Off with thee, Anselmus!" Veronica had grown quite pensive; she spoke no word; only smiled now and then very oddly, and seemed to wish to be left alone. "She, too, has Anselmus in her head," said the Conrector, full of spleen: "but it is well that he does not show himself here; I know he fears me, this Anselmus, and so he will never come.". These concluding words Conrector Paulmann spoke aloud; then the tears rushed into Veronica's eyes, and she said, sobbing: "Ah! how can Anselmus come? He has been corked up in the glass bottle for a long time."

"What? What?" cried Conrector Paulmann. "Ah Heaven! Ah Heaven! she is doting too, like the Registrator: the loud fit will soon come! Ah, you cursed, abominable, thrice-cursed Anselmus!" He ran forth directly to Dr. Eckstein; who smiled, and again said: "Ey! Ey!" This time, however, he prescribed nothing; but added, to the little he had uttered, the following words, as he walked away: "Nerves! Come round of itself. Take the air; walks; amusements; theatre; playing Sonntagskind, Schwestern von Prag. Come around of itself."

"I have seldom seen the Doctor so eloquent," thought Conrector Paulmann; "really talkative, I declare!"

Several days and weeks and months passed. Anselmus had vanished; but Registrator Heerbrand did not make his appearance either: not till the fourth of February, when, in a fashionable new coat of the finest cloth, in shoes and silk stockings, notwithstanding the keen frost, and with a large nosegay of fresh flowers in his hand, the Registrator entered precisely at noon the parlour of Conrector Paulmann, who wondered not a little to see his friend so well dressed. With a solemn air, Registrator Heerbrand came forward to Conrector Paulmann; embraced him with the finest elegance, and then said: "Now at last, on the Saint's-day of your beloved and most honoured Mamsell Veronica, I will tell you out, straightforward, what I have long had lying at my heart. That evening, that unfortunate evening, when I put the ingredients of our noxious punch in my pocket, I intended to tell to you a piece of good news, and to celebrate the happy day in convivial joys. I had learned that I was to be made Hofrath; for which promotion I have now the patent, cum nomine et sigillo Principis, in my pocket."

"Ah! Herr Registr-Herr Hofrath Heerbrand, I meant to say," stammered the Conrector.

"But it is you, most honoured Conrector," continued the new Hofrath; "it is you alone that can complete my happiness. For a long time, I have in secret loved your daughter, Mamsell Veronica; and I can boast of many a kind look which she has given me, evidently showing that she would not reject me. In one word, honoured Conrector! I, Hofrath Heerbrand, do now entreat of you the hand of your most amiable Mamsell Veronica, whom I, if you have nothing against it, purpose shortly to take home as my wife."

Conrector Paulmann, full of astonishment, clapped his hands repeatedly, and cried: "Ey, Ey, Ey! Herr Registr-Herr Hofrath, I meant to say-who would have thought it? Well, if Veronica does really love you, I for my share cannot object: nay, perhaps, her present melancholy is nothing but concealed love for you, most honoured Hofrath! You know what freaks women have!"

At this moment Veronica entered, pale and agitated, as she now commonly was. Then Hofrath Heerbrand approached her; mentioned in a neat speech her Saint's-day, and handed her the odorous nosegay, along with a little packet; out of which, when she opened it, a pair of glittering earrings gleamed up at her. A rapid flying blush tinted her cheeks; her eyes sparkled in joy, and she cried: "O Heaven! These are the very earrings which I wore some weeks ago, and thought so much of."

"How can this be, dearest Mamsell," interrupted Hofrath Heerbrand, somewhat alarmed and hurt, "when I bought them not an hour ago, in the Schlossgasse, for cash?"

But Veronica paid no attention to him; she was standing before the mirror to witness the effect of the trinkets, which she had already suspended in her pretty little ears. Conrector Paulmann disclosed to her, with grave countenance and solemn tone, his friend Heerbrand's preferment and present proposal. Veronica looked at the Hofrath with a searching look, and said: "I have long known that you wished to marry me. Well, be it so! I promise you my heart and hand; but I must now unfold to you, to both of you, I mean, my father and my bridegroom, much that is lying heavy on my heart; yes, even now, though the soup should get cold, which I see Franzchen is just putting on the table."

Without waiting for the Conrector's or the Hofrath's reply, though the words were visibly hovering on the lips of both, Veronica continued: "You may believe me, father, I loved Anselmus from my heart, and when Registrator Heerbrand, who is now become Hofrath himself, assured us that Anselmus might possibly rise that high, I resolved that he arid no other should be my husband. But then it seemed as if alien hostile beings tried snatching him away from me: I had recourse to old Liese, who was once my nurse, but is now a wise woman, and a great enchantress. She promised to help me, and give Anselmus wholly into my hands. We went at midnight on the Equinox to the crossing of the roads: she conjured certain hellish spirits, and by aid of the black cat, we manufactured a little metallic mirror, in which I, directing my thoughts on Anselmus, had but to look, in order to rule him wholly in heart and mind. But now I heartily repent having done all this; and here abjure all Satanic arts. The Salamander has conquered old Liese; I heard her shrieks; but there was no help to be given: so soon as the parrot had eaten the beet, my metallic mirror broke in two with a piercing clang." Veronica took out both the pieces of the mirror, and a lock of hair from her workbox, and handing them to Hofrath Heerbrand, she proceeded: "Here, take the fragments of the mirror, dear Hofrath; throw them down, tonight, at twelve o'clock, over the Elbe Bridge, from the place where the Cross stands; the stream is not frozen there: the lock, however, wear on your faithful breast. I here abjure all magic: and heartily wish Anselmus joy of his good fortune, seeing he is wedded with the green snake, who is much prettier and richer than I. You dear Hofrath, I will love and reverence as becomes a true honest wife."

"Alack! Alack!" cried Conrector Paulmann, full of sorrow; "she is cracked, she is cracked; she can never be Frau Hofräthinn; she is cracked!"

"Not in the smallest," interrupted Hofrath Heerbrand; "I know well that Mamsell Veronica has had some kindness for the loutish Anselmus; and it may be that in some fit of passion, she has had recourse to the wise woman, who, as I perceive, can be no other than the card-caster and coffee-pourer of the Seethor; in a word, old Rauerin. Nor can it be denied that there are secret arts, which exert their influence on men but too banefully; we read of such in the ancients, and doubtless there are still such; but as to what Mamsell Veronica is pleased to say about the victory of the Salamander, and the marriage of Anselmus with the green snake, this, in reality, I take for nothing but a poetic allegory; a sort of song, wherein she sings her entire farewell to the Student."

"Take it for what you will, my dear Hofrath!" cried Veronica; "perhaps for a very stupid dream."

"That I will not do," replied Hofrath Heerbrand; "for I know well that Anselmus himself is possessed by secret powers, which vex him and drive him on to all imaginable mad escapades."

Conrector Paulmann could stand it no longer; he burst out: "Hold! For the love of Heaven, hold! Are we overtaken with that cursed punch again, or has Anselmus's madness come over us too? Herr Hofrath, what stuff is this you are talking? I will suppose, however, that it is love which haunts your brain: this soon comes to rights in marriage; otherwise, I should be apprehensive that you too had fallen into some shade of madness, most honoured Herr Hofrath; then what would become of the future branches of the family, inheriting the malum of their parents? But now I give my paternal blessing to this happy union; and permit you as bride and bridegroom to take a kiss."

This immediately took place; and thus before the soup had grown cold, a formal betrothment was concluded. In a few weeks, Frau Hofräthinn Heerbrand was actually, as she had been in vision, sitting in the balcony of a fine house in the Neumarkt, and looking down with a smile at the beaux, who passing by turned their glasses up to her, and said: "She is a heavenly woman, the Hofräthinn Heerbrand."

Twelfth Vigil

How deeply did I feel, in the centre of my spirit, the blessedness of the Student Anselmus, who now, indissolubly united with his gentle Serpentina, has withdrawn to the mysterious land of wonders, recognized by him as the home towards which his bosom, filled with strange forecastings, had always longed. But in vain was all my striving to set before you, favourable reader, those glories with which Anselmus is encompassed, or even in the faintest degree to shadow them to you in words. Reluctantly I could not but acknowledge the feebleness of my every expression. I felt myself enthralled amid the paltrinesses of everyday life; I sickened in tormenting dissatisfaction; I glided about like a dreamer; in brief, I fell into that condition of the Student Anselmus, which, in the Fourth Vigil, I endeavoured to set before you. It grieved me to the heart, when I glanced over the Eleven Vigils, now happily accomplished, and thought that to insert the Twelfth, the keystone of the whole, would never be permitted me. For whenever, in the night I set myself to complete the work, it was as if mischievous spirits (they might be relations, perhaps cousins-german, of the slain witch) held a polished glittering piece of metal before me, in which I beheld my own mean self, pale, drawn, and melancholic, like Registrator Heerbrand after his bout of punch. Then I threw down my pen, and hastened to bed, that I might behold the happy Anselmus and the fair Serpentina at least in my dreams. This had lasted for several days and nights, when at length quite unexpectedly I received a note from Archivarius Lindhorst, in which he wrote to me as follows:

Respected Sir,-It is well known to me that you have written down, in Eleven Vigils, the singular fortunes of my good son-in-law Anselmus, whilom student, now poet; and are at present cudgelling your brains very sore, that in the Twelfth and Last Vigil you may tell somewhat of his happy life in Atlantis, where he now lives with my daughter, on the pleasant freehold, which I possess in that country. Now, notwithstanding I much regret that hereby my own peculiar nature is unfolded to the reading world; seeing it may, in my office as Privy Archivarius, expose me to a thousand inconveniences; nay, in the Collegium even give rise to the question: How far a Salamander can justly, and with binding consequences, plight himself by oath, as a Servant of the State? and how far, on the whole, important affairs may be intrusted to him, since, according to Gabalis and Swedenborg, the spirits of the elements are not to be trusted at all?--notwithstanding, my best friends must now avoid my embrace; fearing lest, in some sudden anger, I dart out a flash or two, and singe their hair-curls, and Sunday frocks; notwithstanding all this, I say, it is still my purpose to assist you in the completion of the work, since much good of me and of my dear married daughter (would the other two were off my hands also!) has therein been said.

If you would write your Twelfth Vigil, descend your cursed five flights of stairs, leave your garret, and come over to me. In the blue palmtree-room, which you already know, you will find fit writing materials; and you can then, in few words, specify to your readers, what you have seen; a better plan for you than any long-winded description of a life which you know only by hearsay. With esteem.

Your obedient servant.

The Salamander Lindlzorst.

P. T. Royal Archivarius..This somewhat rough, yet on the whole friendly note from Archivarius Lindhorst, gave me high pleasure. It seemed clear enough, indeed, that the singular manner in which the fortunes of his son-in-law had been revealed to me, and which I, bound to silence, must conceal even from you, gracious reader, was well known to this peculiar old gentleman; yet he had not taken it so ill as I might have apprehended. Nay, here was he offering me a helping hand in the completion of my work; and from this I might justly conclude, that at bottom he was not averse to having his marvellous existence in the world of spirits thus divulged through the press.

"It may be," thought I, "that he himself expects from this measure, perhaps, to get his two other daughters married sooner: for who knows but a spark may fall in this or that young man's breast, and kindle a longing for the green snake; whom, on Ascension Day, under the elder-bush, he will forthwith seek and find? From the misery which befell Anselmus, when he was enclosed in the glass bottle, he will take warning to be doubly and trebly on his guard against all doubt and unbelief."

Precisely at eleven o'clock, I extinguished my study lamp; and glided forth to Archivarius Lindhorst, who was already waiting for me in the lobby.

"Are you there, my worthy friend? Well, this is what I like, that you have not mistaken my good intentions: follow me!"

And with this he led the way through the garden, now filled with dazzling brightness, into the azure chamber, where I observed the same violet table, at which Anselmus had been writing.

Archivarius Lindhorst disappeared: but soon came back, carrying in his hand a fair golden goblet, out of which a high blue flame was sparkling up. "Here," said he, "I bring you the favourite drink of your friend the Bandmaster, Johannes Kreisler. It is burning arrack, into which I have thrown a little sugar. Sip a little of it: I will doff my dressing gown, and to amuse myself and enjoy your worthy company while you sit looking and writing, I shall just bob up and down a little in the goblet."

"As you please, honoured Herr Archivarius," answered I: "but if I am to ply the liquor, you will get none."

"Don't fear that, my good fellow," cried the Archivarius; then hastily throwing off his dressing gown, he mounted, to my no small amazement, into the goblet, and vanished in the blaze.

Without fear, softly blowing back the flame, I partook of the drink: it was truly precious!

Stir not the emerald leaves of the palm-trees in soft

sighing and rustling, as if kissed by the breath of the morning wind? Awakened from their sleep, they move, and mysteriously whisper of the wonders, which from the far distance approach like tones of melodious harps! The azure rolls from the walls, and floats like airy vapour to and fro; but dazzling beams shoot through it; and whirling and dancing, as in jubilee of childlike sport, it mounts and mounts to immeasurable height, and vaults over the palm-trees. But brighter and brighter shoots beam upon beam, till in boundless expanse the grove opens where I behold Anselmus. Here glowing hyacinths, and tulips, and roses, lift their fair heads; and their perfumes, in loveliest sound, call to the happy youth: "Wander, wander among us, our beloved; for you understand us! Our perfume is the longing of love: we love you, and are yours for evermore!" The golden rays burn in glowing tones: "We are fire, kindled by love. Perfume is longing; but fire is desire: and do we not dwell in your bosom? We are yours!" The dark bushes, the high trees rustle and sound: "Come to us, beloved, happy one! Fire is desire; but hope is our cool shadow. Lovingly we rustle round your head: for you understand us, because love dwells in your breast!" The brooks and fountains murmur and patter: "Loved one, do not walk so quickly by: look into our crystal! Your image dwells in us, which we preserve with love, for you have understood us." In the triumphal choir, bright birds are singing: "Hear us! Hear us! We are joy, we are delight, the rapture of love!" But anxiously Anselmus turns his eyes to the glorious temple, which rises behind him in the distance.

The fair pillars seem trees; and the capitals and friezes acanthus leaves, which in wondrous wreaths and figures form splendid decorations. Anselmus walks to the Temple: he views with inward delight the variegated marble, the steps with their strange veins of moss. "Ah, no!" cries he, as if in the excess of rapture, "she is not far from me now; she is near!" Then Serpentina advances, in the fullness of beauty and grace, from the Temple; she bears the Golden Flower Pot, from which a bright lily has sprung. The nameless rapture of infinite longing glows in her meek eyes; she looks at Anselmus, and says: "Ah! Dearest, the Lily has opened her blossom: what we longed for is fulfilled; is there a happiness to equal ours?" Anselmus clasps her with the tenderness of warmest ardour: the lily burns in flaming beams over his head. And louder move the trees and bushes; clearer and gladder play the brooks; the birds, the shining insects dance in the waves of perfume: a gay, bright rejoicing tumult, in the air, in the water, in the earth, is holding the festival of love! Now sparkling streaks rush, gleaming over all the bushes; diamonds look from the ground like shining eyes: strange vapours are wafted hither on sounding wings: they are the spirits of the elements, who do homage to the lily, and proclaim the happiness of Anselmus. Then Anselmus raises his head, as if encircled with a beamy glory. Is it looks? Is it words? Is it song? You hear the sound: "Serpentina! Belief in you, love of you has unfolded to my soul the inmost spirit of nature! You have brought me the lily, which sprang from gold, from the primeval force of the world, before

Phosphorus had kindled the spark of thought; this lily is knowledge of the sacred harmony of all beings; and in this I live in highest blessedness for evermore. Yes, I, thrice happy, have perceived what was highest: I must indeed love thee forever, O Serpentina! Never shall the golden blossoms of the lily grow pale; for, like belief and love, this knowledge is eternal."

For the vision, in which I had now beheld Anselmus bodily, in his freehold of Atlantis, I stand indebted to the arts of the Salamander; and it was fortunate that when everything had melted into air, I found a paper lying on the violet-table, with the foregoing statement of the matter, written fairly and distinctly by my own hand. But now I felt myself as if transpierced and torn in pieces by sharp sorrow. "Ah, happy Anselmus, who has cast away the burden of everyday life, who in the love of kind Serpentina flies with bold pinion, and now lives in rapture and joy on your freehold in Atlantis! while I-poor I!-must soon, nay, in few moments, leave even this fair hall, which itself is far from a Freehold in Atlantis; and again be transplanted to my garret, where, enthralled among the pettinesses of existence, my heart and my sight are so bedimmed with thousand mischiefs, as with thick fog, that the fair lily will never, never be beheld by me."

Then Archivarius Lindhorst patted me gently on the shoulder, and said: "Softly, softly, my honoured friend! Do not lament so! Were you not even now in Atlantis; and have you not at least a pretty little copyhold farm there, as the poetical possession of your inward sense? And is the blessedness of

Anselmus anything else but a living in poesy? Can anything else but poesy reveal itself as the sacred harmony of all beings, as the deepest secret of nature?"

THE END

www.ingramcontent.com/pod-product-compliance
Lightning Source LLC
Chambersburg PA
CBHW030338020726
47493CB00004B/1314